CHEMICAL
ATTRACTION

CHEMICAL ATTRACTION

MIKE UDEN

THAMES RIVER PRESS

Chemical Attraction

THAMES RIVER PRESS
An imprint of Wimbledon Publishing Company Limited (WPC)
Another imprint of WPC is Anthem Press (www.anthempress.com)
First published in the United Kingdom in 2013 by
THAMES RIVER PRESS
75–76 Blackfriars Road
London SE1 8HA

www.thamesriverpress.com

A CIP record for this book is available from the British Library.

ISBN 978-1-78308-165-3

This title is also available as an eBook

To Jan

CHEMICAL ATTRACTION

MIKE UDEN

Ben

I suppose it all started, or perhaps ended, that weekend. The agency bar was rocking. Apparently we'd won some big account or other. Friday, free booze – a winner.

On the way through, Ned (he's my copywriting partner) and I bid a few high-fives to the other lads – all jeans around their arses and cardigans – necked a couple of Stripes, made for the gent's, shared a line and returned to the bar. We then tried our luck with a couple of junior execs – upright collars, pointy tits – failed, left and hailed a cab for Soho.

I suppose it was about nine by the time we got to our club, media mostly, a bit wanky: all trilbies and vests. We drank another half dozen beers, staggered to a nearby Thai, ate curry, drank more beer and cabbed it back to Ned's. More booze, more charlie, add some dope, collapse. Like I said; a real winner.

Saturday started late, with a pain in my head and a ringtone in my ear. *Can't be Monday, can it?*

I groped for the phone: 'Wake up,' said Ned, 'Groundhog night!'

So we pubbed and we partied all over again. Except for one big difference. I managed to cop off with a girl from another agency called Abbie. That was her name, not the agency's. At least, I think it was. Whatever; she probably can't remember my name either.

On Sunday, I had a long lie-in, went round to Ned's, met more friends and repeated the performance. Minus the sex, but plus the vomit. Great weekend.

Monday morning, unsurprisingly, I felt like cold shit: gurgling guts and bubbling bowel. Between toilet visits (both ends) I showered, pulled on a few clothes and made for work.

When I got to the station, pausing for deep breaths on the way, it was well past rush hour and the platform was nearly empty. Thank god.

The train turned up: strobing lights, lurching carriages, and seats of puce and peacock. I felt even worse, if that's possible. I leaned forward, put my head in my hands and swayed with the train. Worse still. So I took my hands from my head, leaned back and opened my eyes. No better.

There were free newspapers strewn everywhere and, from somewhere down the carriage, an empty can was rolling back and forth, mocking me: roll, stop, pause — back, stop, pause. I closed my eyes again. Nope. Leaned back. Still nope. Eyes open, eyes closed, any position, feel shit.

After about ten nauseous minutes a voice said: *Baker Street. This is Baker Street.* I stood up, swayed and almost fell over – the train's fault, not mine. I breathed in and stepped out. As the train left, I just stood there, back to moving carriage, eyes closed. Warm, underground stench.

I stumbled through tunnels, under vicious lights, and found the escalator. Slowly, we rose. At the top, I lurched forward, stuffed my ticket into the slot and the jaws opened. A few steps and I was out. Bright and breezy, noise everywhere. Even worse.

After a short distance I found a bench and sat. Work was only metres away but it might as well have been miles.

I must have dozed off because when I opened my eyes I was lying across the bench, my mouth was dry and saliva had dribbled down my shirt. I straightened myself up and yawned. A passerby gave me a look, probably thought I was some kind of pisshead.

By the time I'd dragged myself through the agency's doors it was gone twelve-thirty. Some of the perkier types were already on their way out for lunch.

'Ah, Ben, you're wanted in Tiny's office,' said Trudy, our glammed-up receptionist.

This seemed a little odd. Creative Director, is Tiny. My boss. He didn't normally do Monday morning meetings. Then again it wasn't morning, I suppose. I could've done without it, though. Oh well, probably nothing too heavy.

I took the silent lift to the fifth floor with a couple of blokes from finance. I only half knew them. In a small lift, when you're next to people you wouldn't normally speak to, it's difficult to know where to look. Especially if you smell of sick. So I looked down at my trainers. They were odd.

Seventh floor. I got out, walked down the carpeted corridor and pushed through the doors. Sadie was there. She's the girl who protects Tiny.

'Ah, Ben,' she said, in the same, slightly worrying tone as the receptionist. 'Take a seat.'

I slumped down and looked towards Tiny's door. It was closed. Abnormal.

Then Petronella walked in. She's HR. She went straight past Sadie, straight past me and straight into Tiny's. And closed the door again. Then a couple of blokes in suits did the same thing. Who the fuck are they?

Closed doors. What's with these closed doors?

I leafed through an old *Campaign* but it made me feel sick again, so I slung it back, slumped back and closed my eyes.

I must have started to doze because I was suddenly jolted awake by the phone on Sadie's desk.

She picked it up, looked towards me and, *Apprentice*-style, said: 'Tiny will see you now.'

So I pushed myself up and made for the door. I'm not really accustomed to closed doors, so even though I'd been told I could enter, I paused.

'Come in,' said Tiny's voice from within.

So I went in. On the far side of his table, seated to his left, were Petronella and the two unknown suits.

'These are company solicitors,' said Tiny, telling me their now-forgotten names. 'Oh,' he added, 'and you know Petronella, don't you. Please take a seat.'

'Hi,' is all I said, pulling up a chair.

I can't imagine what they thought of me, but I didn't greatly care. Creatives are supposed to be scruffy, aren't they?

'Ben,' he said, perhaps a little patronizingly. 'You're aware that we had a pitch this morning – for KemiKlene, I mean?'

Actually, I'd completely forgotten. Frankly, I couldn't have pitched a fucking tent, let alone a campaign.

Then it all slowly came back to me. That Friday, before the piss-ups and the partying, Ned and I had been working on a new spot for TrueLoo. TrueLoo is KemiKlene's new wonder toilet cleaner, by the way. We were trying to come up with a decent idea and getting absolutely nowhere. I do remember Ned asking me why we had to make a big deal about the germs *under* the rim – the ones you can't see. In Ned's opinion, if you can't see them, how the fuck would you know it's worked? Fair enough, I suppose.

But I told him that that was the whole point. You had to squirt and squirt as if your life depended on it, that way we sell more. Ned said it's immoral. I replied: it's advertising.

So given KemiKlene were unlikely to accept something along the lines of *TrueLoo. It might not work*, or *TrueLoo. It's immoral*, we'd failed to come up with fuck all.

So off to the bar we'd gone.

'All the other teams came up with stuff,' snapped Tiny. 'Why didn't you?'

I couldn't think of an answer. In fact, I couldn't think of anything. Except my bowels.

Then, slowly and smugly, he listed the stuff the other teams had done: the PowerPoints; the storyboards; the spreadsheets. He said everyone had worked round the clock – that all four teams had produced 'bloody good pitches'. Except us.

'So what was your idea?' he asked.

My mind was blank. I wondered if Ned would have been given a similar bollocking, but I doubted it. Okay, he'd probably get a grilling, but no more. You see, he wouldn't have been über late for a start. And more importantly, his face fits. Mine didn't. I had history too. I was already on a yellow card for insulting the Bendy Burger clients. That's the agency's second biggest account – to KemiKlene.

Sweating, head pounding, I needed to come up with an idea. Pronto. I remembered the plastic aerosols that we'd stuck on our office desk. We'd used them as goal posts. You know, lobbing bits of paper at them – crumpled up scripts and stuff. We'd already downed a few lagers. And from memory – very, very vague memory – the packs were Lemon Fresh and Original Blue.

An idea hit me.

'Blue,' I mumbled, looking down at my fingers.

I looked up. They were all looking back at me. Four monkeys. All equally confused.

'Blue,' I repeated.

'Blue?' replied Tiny. 'What about blue?'

'It's blue isn't it? The liquid, I mean.'

'The Original, yes,' he confirmed.

'That's my idea, then: Blue.'

This seemed to completely confuse them.

'Blue?'

'Yes. The whole campaign, based on blue. You know, a bluesy track, a cool guy, a foxy chick.'

'Cleaning the toilet?' asked Petronella.

She was probably more accustomed to HR meetings than creative ones – wasn't used to the abstraction.

'Yeah, why not?' I replied. 'With blue-tinted footage. You know, moody, cool – and erm, well – *blue*.'

Why the fuck I hadn't come up with this before? It was bloody brilliant. Maybe Ned and I should get pissed more. There again, that would be almost impossible.

'So that's your presentation is it?' said Tiny. 'Just the word *Blue*?'

'Well, not only, no'

There was a silence, a sort of long pause. I had nothing to add.

'So come on,' he snapped, 'what else have you got?'

I looked down again, away from their gaze.

'Did you brief the account team with this brilliant *Blue* idea?' This time he sort of sneered the word.

'Erm, no.'

'Did you do a storyboard?'

I shook my head.

'Mood edit?'

I shrugged. No mood edit. Obviously.

'Tell you what,' he said. 'Forget the mood edit, forget the bloody storyboard, have you given this *any* previous thought at all?'

I sat in silence.

He coughed – a little affectedly, I thought – then said: 'I'm afraid, Ben,' then he leant back on his chair, 'we're going to have to let you go.'

'*Blue-loo*,' I crooned quietly – you know, almost at a whisper. '*You saw me sitting alone.*'

'You what?' he interrupted.

'That would be the music.' I said 'You know... *Blue Loo, you saw me sit ...*'

'I heard you the first fucking time!' he barked.

He then jumped to his feet and almost screamed; completely lost it: 'Aren't you fucking listening? You're fucking fired. Do you understand me? *Fired.*'

Petronella looked a little concerned. I guess phrases with the word fuck in them are frowned upon in HR circles. They probably prefer: 'We need to consider our downsizing options', or: 'We're rationalising our headcount situation'.

Oh well, I thought. In for a penny. You see, I still thought it was a good idea... '*Blue-oo Loo... la la la la la - la la...*'

Tiny almost bust a blood vessel, stabbing his finger: 'Forget Blue Sodding Loo, forget Cunting KemiKlene, forget advertising, in fact. You're fucking toast.' He then pointed to the door and screamed: 'Now fuck off out of it, and don't come back.'

Petronella went white.

Was I surprised? Was I distraught? Well, not overly. I was just horribly, viciously, savagely hung over. And hangovers take precedence over everything, don't they? Nothing else really matters. That's the whole point, isn't it? Why get pissed if things still matter?

All I really wanted to do was curl up and sleep.

Fuck Tiny. Fuck KemiKlene. Fuck advertising.

Lily

TEFL's been good to me. That's *Teaching English as a Foreign Language*. I've seen the world, or most of it, and been paid for the privilege – and it *has* been a privilege. Bangkok, Beijing, Rio, it always starts with an exchange of emails, followed by a cheap flight, then into a dusty old bus or a rusty old taxi and then, exhaustedly, a backpack collapse onto a sagging bed in some simple digs. I might then meet some other teachers – Australians or Canadians or Irish and then, as soon as the jetlag abates, it's into the classroom; a setting so familiar you could almost taste it. You see, for some reason, TEFL classrooms often seem to hark back to some long gone Jean Brodie model – old desks, beige walls and blackboards – but are filled with happy, jabbering kids, doing their best, mouthing their phonemics, reciting their verbs. Wonderful.

There's a downside, of course. Money. Or the lack of it. As a TEFL teacher, you'll never be rich and, because of that and because of the traveling, you'll never really have roots either. Certainly not roots you could call your own, anyway.

I've always loved English. Loved its precision and its ambiguity, its truth and its lies. You can do all that with English, and more. I love reading it, writing it and that's why, I suppose, I love teaching it. So love all round, then? Well, not entirely, no. You see, in a way, this is really why the whole thing started.

At the time, I was working the TEFL schools in London, beavering away, saving up for my next trip. But when the week was over, when I'd cleaned the final board on a Friday, there was always this gap. A gap that no amount of third conditionals or non-defining relative clauses could fill.

Colleagues always said I was the steady one, the reliable one. Always on time, always dependable. And I suppose I still am. But reliable and dependable aren't the same as lovable, are they? And, if you'll excuse another linguistic pun, being steady isn't the same thing as going steady, is it?

I always thought of my work, and therefore my life (because that's all I had), as being like a steady, disciplined swim. You know, like a purposeful front crawl down one of those long, straight lanes they have at the local swimming pool. Monday to Friday, length after length, head down, just keep going; reading, writing, grammar – stroke, stroke, breathe. And when I was finished, when I got to Friday, it was like that glow you feel after you've showered and toweled – a good job, well done.

But like I said earlier, it wasn't perfect, not quite. There was still something missing. What am I saying, *something*? It wasn't something, it was *someone*. Someone to ruffle up my precision a little. Someone to do something a little different – take me out of myself.

It was a Friday and, being a caring sort of person (in my opinion, anyway), I used to buy a copy of *The Big Issue* from the man outside the Wimpy bar. Rather sad and hollow-eyed, he was. You see, on my wages, I couldn't really afford to donate much to charities, so it was my way – my tiny way – of helping. I didn't tend to read it; in fact I often left it on the bus. But not this time. This time, when the bus arrived, I settled into my seat next to a window – all graffiti-etched, as I recall – and put it in my bag. I needed to get some work done, so I started looking at the homework I had to mark ('write about an incident from your childhood using narrative tenses'). This was because, that particular Friday, I had a date.

My normal Friday, my perfect, unruffled, predictable Friday, consisted of a decent book, a glass of wine and a veggie takeaway. Oh, and once I'd put my tray down, McFlurry, my big white cat, would jump up and sort of knead at me. Actually he wasn't mine. He belonged two doors down the corridor. But he was a bit of a tart on the kneading front.

In fact, one of my jokes was that McFlurry was the only living being, in the whole wide world, that kneaded me. I would tell that joke to my teacher friends – typically TEFL-esque – you know, wordplay. But it did have a grain of truth in it. Like I said – there was definitely something missing.

But that particular Friday, to McFlurry's disgust (who sat resentfully in the corner with eyes narrowed and tail flicking), I was showering and blow-drying like the best of 'em.

It wasn't the first time I'd plucked up the courage to use Datadate. Apparently you can find Internet dating sites now for just about anything nowadays. No-strings sites, no-names sites. I'm only surprised there's not a no-show site. Stood-up Dot Com.

All I wanted was a little bit of love.

I was a little wary of using them, to be honest. It wasn't so much the dangers, real or perceived, but because I'd found the whole process to be so, so wearisome. Not the blokes necessarily, some of whom had been quite dishy – and not because I had problems with men, as such. It was just that the whole thing was so, well, contrived. Sort of like an interview, really.

By the time you'd met your date they'd checked your Facebook, read your CV and knew pretty much everything. Most blokes were looking for lifelong partnerships or marriage and, in many cases, families. All of which was great, but rather clinical. Form filling, box ticking. Boys looking for egg donors, girls for sperm wranglers. Fecundity certificates, anyone?

Okay, I'm thirty, not fifteen, but shouldn't there be a few butterflies and giggles? You know, a bit of romance?

I had known love, albeit nine years earlier. Achingly authentic, all consuming – the real deal. That was at uni and that was Adam. Beautiful Adam – my lover, my soul mate, my life-companion – or so I thought. But life at uni isn't real life, and when Adam went backpacking, I stayed back. And from the distance, it all just died. I realize now that I stayed in education – Celta, Delta, PGCE – not just to learn lots, and certainly not to earn lots, but because, in a way, it was a cop-out. An ultimate lack of decision-making. It's also the ultimate indulgence.

Sitting there, like a baby sparrow, being fed and fed. Eventually, using my English qualifications, it was me that did the travelling. But not before Adam came back, meeting and marrying a girl in Crawley, East Sussex and working, ironically, at Gatwick Airport.

So with the bloke next door being a Morris Dancer, the postman gay and my fellow teachers, well, fellow teachers, it was all down to the Internet. And there I was, in the black trouser suit I'd rejected as way too smart an hour earlier, pouting at the mirror for a final lippy check and tousling my hair for a final bit of bounce.

I'm not really sure why I bothered. After a drizzly walk through south London, and a windswept wait on the station, I looked at my reflection in the (locked) waiting room window and I was back where I started. Teacher again. Glamour to grammar.

But then, once I got off the train at London Bridge and started walking to our chosen venue, my mood changed. Don't be such a misery, I said to myself. This could be the one. After all, he looked okay on Datadate *and* he seemed to have the same interests – books and travelling. So yes, this could be it. Dave, the man I would share my whole life with.

I recognized him the minute I walked into the pub. He had the same eager face and the same expectant eyes that had been peering out of my desktop for the previous three weeks. Like meeting someone's homepage. Except it wasn't.

A goatee! Where did that come from? And how old did that make the photo? Unless he'd airbrushed it. The photo, I mean, not his face. There again, looking at it...

I'm not a fan of goatees. Except on goats, of course. Anyway, after a panted hello and a damp handshake, he guided me to the corner table he'd been guarding (for the past half hour, according to him), but in an instant it was gone. Not the goatee, sadly, but the table. Apparently, in his enthusiasm to meet me he'd vacated his hard-won space at such haste that another couple had snuck in behind him. So what with the bumfluff beard, the wet handshake and the lack of masculine territory defending, not a great start.

With no seat readily available, he ushered me to the bar and tried to attract the barman's attention, whilst simultaneously attempting to hold an over-the-shoulder conversation with me. He failed on all counts, so I suppose he did manage to demonstrate his masculinity via one male trait – a total failure to be able to do more than one thing at once. So I took over the drink-ordering responsibilities and attracted a barman's attention instantly. The extra undone button probably helped.

Refreshments sorted, and with me, rather than he, managing to find a replacement table, we sat down. Oh yes, and we were squeezed between an Afrikaans-speaking couple and a piss-smelling toilet.

Originally, we'd chosen this particular Bankside pub because London Bridge station was convenient for both of us (me from Lewisham on BR, he from Barnet on the Northern Line) and in truth it should have been a romantic setting – offering views of the Thames flowing darkly below the silhouetted St Paul's. But we found ourselves sitting next to each other, rather than opposite, staring at a blank wall, rather than a view, and listening to the world's most grating accent, rather than our own voices. Oh yes, and almost gagging on the smell of stale piss.

Eventually, the couple left and, face-to-face, we had the table to ourselves. This should have loosened things up, and allowed us to get to know each other better. Well, we got to know each other. But 'better' wouldn't necessarily be the adjective.

His main reading interests, according to his posting, were modern classics. Perfect.

But as we talked about authors (his idea, not mine – I'd happily have chatted about anything) I got the distinct impression he'd been swatting up especially for this date. For instance, his favourite British author, George Orwell, was 'named after a River in Ipswich'. His favourite American author, John Steinbeck, was 'interested in submarines'. And his all-time fave, Ernest Hemingway, 'drove a black Buick'. All of which had absolutely nothing to do with literature, and had a distinct whiff of Wiki about it.

Why do blokes do it? Why pretend you're something you're not? Did he think I was going to jump into bed with him? Did he think I was going to have his babies? All because of his extensive knowledge of Alexander Solzhenitsyn's record collection? Oh yes and on the subject of music, his favourite band was the distinctly un-classic Slipknot – and, around his wrist, he had a grimy collection of those identity bracelets they give you at gigs. A sudden shiver went through me. Given that one of them appeared to be made of paper, he must A) never wash, or B) take them off when he showers. I'm not sure which was the least appealing: aquaphobe or anorak – like a cub scout with his dirty little, much-fingered, never-taken-off toggle.

So having established that we had absolutely bugger all in common, the conversation petered out into stilted silences. He then asked me if I wanted another drink (I was desperate, but not that desperate) and then if I was hungry (ditto). I looked at my watch and, after a silent pause, he coughed. I said I really should be getting back – the trains to Lewisham were bad that night (lie) and stood up. So he stood up, mumbled something about keeping in touch; I coughed 'mmm', which he could take as 'yes' but was certainly 'no', and said goodbye. He then said 'Yo' (or some such) and, as I was pulling on my coat, gave me two pecks: one sideswiping my sleeve, the other wetting my face.

Mercifully, that was that. Ordeal over. For both of us.

I walked through the empty streets of Borough Market with cobblestones jarring my heels and stood for twenty minutes on a freezing platform. When a train eventually arrived I found myself in a customary Friday night carriage, full of drunken vomiters migrating south. I alighted at an empty Lewisham station and hurried back down darkened streets from whence I came – past groups of leering and (I imagined) flick-knifed youths.

I breathed a giant sigh of relief when I rounded the corner into my street and was jangling my keys well before I reached my door. I almost fell into my flat and then collapsed directly into my chair – just in time for McFlurry to jump up and greet me with his little circular clawing dance. After a bit of mutual kneading I got up, made a toasted cheese sandwich, poured myself a glass of wine and settled back down in the chair again. A normal, if delayed, Friday night. Thank God. It was then that I noticed the *Big Issue* I'd put down just before going out.

I picked it up and saw an advertisement for a company called MediSee: '*Volunteers for Clinical Trials required*' said the ad. '*Make a valuable contribution to medical research and get paid in the process!*' Interesting, I thought. '*We at MediSee represent ethically sound drug companies*' (bit of an oxymoron, but hey ho!). I read on: '*Earn up to three thousand pounds in your spare time.*' Then there were some pictures of happy young people, playing pool, chatting to each other and generally having a good time. '*You'll be working with experienced doctors and nurses in a friendly, relaxed environment in one of London's top teaching hospitals. Do your bit for medicine and get paid in the process!*' Then it gave some contact details before signing of with: '*Join the MediSee team now!*'

Exit strategy? Round-the-world nest egg? Goodbye to grey skies and goatees? It's a thought.

Ben

'I can't believe it!' said Ned, psycho eyes, nostrils flaring. 'The fucking bastards!'

'Yeah,' I agreed.

It was Friday evening and a working week, or non-working, had already passed by.

We were standing in the Hoxton Hope – early doors, beers untouched – and over the previous twenty minutes I'd been recounting events as coolly and dispassionately as I could. Ned had been playing the supporting role: consoling words, shaking head, exasperated looks. He even suggested resigning from the agency himself, to which I told him not to be so bloody stupid. After all, he had a mortgage too.

'Yeah, talking of which,' he replied, 'what the fuck are you gonna do for money?'

I simply shrugged. I knew the maths. Outgoings: mortgage, council tax and utilities. Two-and-a-half a month. And that was without the things that made life worth living. Incomings: zero. Savings: zero. Credit cards: discredited.

'Don't worry,' I said, not even convincing myself. 'Something'll turn up, no worries.'

What bollocks. There was nothing out there.

'One month's wages, that's all they gave me,' I recounted for the umpteenth time. 'Even took my fucking phone.'

'Tell you what,' said Ned, perking up a bit, taking a swig of beer. 'You know that geezer that used to work in the print department. Gormless, dangly earrings, Chelsea tosser.'

I thought for a second. Couldn't recall anyone of that description.

'Tom, I think. Yes, that was his name.'

Still couldn't picture him. Too wound up in my own problems. I just said yes anyway.

You know what he did? After he lost his job, to earn a few bob, I mean.'

'Rent boy?'

'Did some medical tests. Paul was telling me – you know Paul from IT, don't you.'

I couldn't recall Paul from IT either. I just said yes again.

'He did this medicine stuff. This bloke Tom, I mean. Piece of piss, apparently. All you do is turn up and take some drugs.'

'Sounds like this place,' I replied, looking round the pub.

'Yeah, but they don't pay you three grand for doing it.'

'Three grand.'

'Yeah, three grand.'

It sounded interesting, so we discussed it. And having said what a great wheeze it was, Ned then put the dampener on it by telling me that a few years back some bloke had lost his fingers doing it. To which I made some remark about costing an arm and a leg. Anyway, enough of all that. We changed subjects, the night wore on and it all got a bit messy: drinks in Soho (only for networking purposes), a terrifying club in New Cross (God knows how we got south of the river), a dead kebab from Peckham and a minicab from hell.

As Ned stumbled out, insisting he should pay – handing a handful of coins and crumpled notes to the driver – he put his arm round me, kissed me on the cheek and slurred: 'Don't forgeh tha' medshon shtuf.'

'Yeah, yeah,' I said. 'I'll Google 'em. I promish.'

CalmerCeutical Ltd.

For William Wyles, CEO of CalmerCeutical, his work was everything: his baby, his lover, his life. So the longer he could delay going home to the bosom of his young (second) family the better – particularly on a Friday night, for the commencement of another unappealing weekend of Range Rovers, bouncy castles and Chicken McNuggets. The simple solution was to schedule end-of-week meetings as late as possible and, to this end, he'd asked Amraj, his Chief Scientific Officer, to be in his office at six-thirty prompt to discuss their latest drug trials.

And at exactly that time, Michelle, Wyles's secretary, knocked on the door and ushered Amraj in. She then went off to prepare some beer and nibbles whilst the men exchanged pleasantries about what they'd be doing at the weekend.

A few minutes later Michelle came back in with a tray full of goodies, poured their beers and left.

Once she'd gone, the small talk finished, Wyles looked down at the notes and the meeting proper began: 'Well here goes then. We're off.'

'Yup,' agreed Amraj. 'Let's hope it's successful.'

'It certainly should be, you've worked hard enough,' assured Wyles, as winter rain streaked the black windows behind him. 'Anyway,' he shrugged, 'the animal data's promising and the human safety stuff looks good too, so there shouldn't be any problems.'

'Touch wood,' said Amraj, putting his hand on his boss's laminate desk.

In a way the hard work was indeed behind them. The funding had been raised some two years back, then came the quality testing, then the efficacy tests – on little pink rats – and now? The big one: the first tests on humans. Having established the drug's efficacy on animals, the next stage was to check its safety on humans. And by subcontracting their clinical trials to MediSee – an expert in the field – they would be able to establish just that. Quality, Safety, Efficacy: the very mantra of the pharmaceutical industry.

'So here's to PC352,' proposed Wyles, raising his drink.

'Pheroxosol,' countered Amraj, raising his.

'Is that our working title?'

'Why not?' he shrugged.

'Okay, to Pheroxosol,' nodded Wyles, 'the first anti-depressant with absolutely no side effects.'

'Let's hope so,' agreed Amraj.

Briefly, they looked at each other. Neither wanted to be the first to say what they were thinking. Whilst they both knew that it might not have some of the habit-forming nastiness of other drugs, they also knew that there was a possibility, the slightest of chances, that there could be an entirely different side effect to PC352.

The little pink rats for instance, apart from possibly being less chaotic – which was what you'd expect – seemed to fight less and copulate more. This proved little though. Calm animals were more likely to have sex than anxious animals. And nothing in the make-up of the early form of the drug suggested, in the accepted sense, that it was an aphrodisiac. No, the reason why they had this hunch was because Amraj had shared his thoughts with his boss about this drug from its very inception.

Back then, Wyles hadn't been that interested. Primarily, he was a businessman, not a scientist. Anti-depressants made good business sense. Love potions, as he put it, didn't. But the more Amraj had told him about it, the more curious he'd become.

'There's nothing unnatural about this stuff,' Amraj had told him, over a celebratory post-rodent trial biryani. 'We've already got it inside us.'

'Doesn't necessarily make it good,' replied Wyles, leaning back and slapping his belly.

'No,' said Amraj, taking his point. 'But we're talking chemicals, not curry.'

Apart from a chin-on-his-chest burp, Wyles failed to react to this, so Amraj just ploughed on: 'Pregnant women produce it – oxytocin I mean. It bonds them with their baby *and* helps them sleep.'

Wyles wasn't that interested in pregnant woman, though sleep sounded like a good idea.

Amraj looked down at his boss's rather expectant belly and did consider making an obvious comment, but thought better of it. So he just went into a rather boring account of how oxytocin had originally been tested on autistic children.

'Because it reduces shyness, you see,' he said. 'It increases eye contact and stuff too. But it seems to work for pretty much everyone. You know, helps people meet and then, well, it improves intimacy… when they finally get round to, well…'

'During or after?' joked Wyles, not knowing much about intimacy at all.

'Both,' said Amraj.

'So let's get this straight,' said Wyles, his eyes briefly closed. 'Having shagged yourself senseless, you fancy a snooze – just like a bloke. But you also fancy a cuddle, like a tart?'

Amraj had never quite thought of it like this before, but yes, this little cocktail *could* possibly bring the sexes together more.

'Maybe,' shrugged Amraj. 'I mean, in the tests it *increased* sexual activity – in the rats, I mean – but *reduced* their number of sexual partners.'

'So more sex, but more faithful too,' said Wyles, calling for the bill. 'Interesting.'

'Yes,' said Amraj. 'It's the oxytocin, you see, but we've got pheromones in there too.'

'Where do they come in?'

'Well, for us, reducing stress, but they also come into the whole sexual attraction thing. *And then* there's the dopamine – the "reward" drug,' he said, drawing quotation marks.

'Reward?'

'Yes, it's called that because it makes you want more. Most illegal substances produce it, but so does… well, put it this way: during sex your brain gets flooded with the stuff.'

'Not in my case,' joked Wyles. 'But seriously, you're saying that all the stuff we're putting in our anti-depressants could also improve relationships?'

'Yes. The dating, the getting together *and* the staying together.'

Driving back to the office that night, while his CSO droned on and on about research, Wyles found himself thinking and thinking.

'And this stuff will be simple to use too?'

'Er, yes, a nasal spray… oh yes, talking of which, my research threw up something else too… about pheromones, I mean.'

'What's that?' said Wyles, opening the glove and taking out some Tic Tacs.

'Well, you know that they're all tied up with our sense of smell.'

Wyles knocked back the mints and offered them to Amraj.

'Thanks,' said Amraj. 'But do you know pheromones are actually *for?*'

'Make us smell nicer?' crunched Wyles.

'Well, yes, but apart from that they seem to back up that old adage: opposites attract.'

'How's that?'

'Like most things, it's evolutionary. Pheromones help us find someone who is completely *different* to us.'

'So that's why Celia smells different to me, you mean?'

'Exactly. If you smell different you *are* different – and mixed genes mean survival. For the next generation, that is.'

'I still don't quite see how that works. I mean, most blokes would shag anything, irrespective of its smell.'

'Aha!' said Amraj. 'But the few women they *wouldn't*, er, shag – mothers, daughters, sisters – exactly proves my point. Close relatives have close genes, so they smell the same!'

'So I don't fancy my Mum because I smell like her?' he said.

'Well, yes... I mean, no...' stuttered Amraj.

Whatever, thought Wyles. All he could really think about was PC352's – sorry, Pheroxosol's – hidden potential and the term Amraj had used to describe it. But for Wyles, *reward drug* had an entirely different meaning.

Lily

In a way, it felt like I'd won something. A prize or a competition, maybe. After all, not everyone who applies is chosen, or so I'm told. I'd filled in the online application form – during which time I'd told them that no, I didn't suffer from psoriasis, piles or irritable bowel syndrome, but did admit to poor sleep and the occasional anxiety attack. They promised they'd send me another form to fill in, which duly arrived a week or so later. On this I had to sign a disclaimer, as well as give assurances that I had no sexually transmitted diseases and wasn't pregnant. Assurances! I could give them copper-bottomed guarantees. Unless McFlurry had kneaded his way into my womb.

So I sent that off, and had kind of put it to the back of my mind when an envelope appeared on mat with the name MediSee emblazoned across it. I opened it, sort of assuming I'd been rejected.

It gave nothing away to start with; no 'congratulations' or 'you've been chosen' or anything like that, just a note informing me that I'd been short-listed pending an informal interview. It almost sounded like a job application. Or perhaps a submission for an online dating agency. Anyway, they gave me a couple of options for the meeting, so I rang them and plumped for the following Friday.

I was so excited that I rang Suzie. She's my best friend. Actually, that's not entirely true, she's my *only* friend. Sad isn't it? Not so much the only friend thing, but the fact that I actually get excited about an interview for a clinical trial. Oh well, life in the fast lane. The only other person I made up my mind to tell was Jen. She's my sister. But I've got to sort of prepare myself for that one. It's not that we don't get on. It's more that, no matter what age you are, big sisters remain big sisters. Oh yes, and I'd love to have told Mum and Dad, but they'd only worry. And if I'm truthful, that was my other emotion: Worry.

You see, after I'd sent the initial application form, I did do a bit of research on clinical trials. If you Google 'clinical trials' you get loads of ads for companies like MediSee. But if you Google 'clinical trials' and then 'disasters', you get a load of really scary stuff about trials that went horribly wrong. Then again, if you researched 'maypole dancing in Reigate' and then threw in the word 'disasters' you'd probably get some pretty grim stuff there too. So I thought, what the heck, the worst they can do is turn me into a vegetable and my life isn't exactly carnivorous at the moment anyway. So I went for it.

As it turned out, MediSee is based at St Thomas's, which was kind of reassuring. You feel far happier about entrusting your body parts to a company that is run from such a famous hospital, don't you?

I took the train there – it's an easy journey from Lewisham to Waterloo (out of the rush hour, that is) – and arrived ten minutes early. I found a seat in a light, airy reception area, thumbed through a couple of magazines and was soon greeted and shown around by a kind-faced yet efficient nurse called Angela Harty. On my brief tour I saw offices, labs and wards – some of which had private rooms – and everything hummed with a welcoming efficiency. I'm really going to like this, I thought.

The interview was really relaxed – so nothing like a first date after all – and only lasted about twenty minutes (which perhaps, *is* more like a first date, or at least one of *my* first dates). They told me I'd be taking medication four times a day – twice in the morning, once at lunchtime and once before bed. After the morning and lunchtime doses, various tests would be done for blood, urine and saliva – that's for stress levels apparently – and after the nighttime dose I'd just sleep, hopefully. Actually, as

I'd kind of guessed, the main purpose of the drug – which was called Pheroxosol, by the way – was to keep you relaxed, help you sleep, and make you, well… a nicer person. Better and better. Paid to be nice.

Oh yes, there'd be no injections – I hate injections – and in my case, being a girl, if I wanted to – which I did – I could have a private room. I could definitely do without two weeks of farting, snoring blokes.

There were some other things I hadn't realized either. I knew the drug had already been tested for safety, but I didn't know that safety tests were generally only done on men. Only after that, for quality and efficacy, are drugs tested on men *and* women. Quite right, too. If people are going to have bits falling off their bodies, it should certainly be male bits. And as for quality, if that's what they're testing, *obviously* it needs to be on women, doesn't it?

Another thing I hadn't realized was that the tests would be what they call 'double blind'. This means that some of us will get placebos and some won't, but, more to the point, we won't know who's got what – and neither will the clinicians giving me the medication. Only the people gathering the results will know. Well as long as someone does, frankly my dear… Actually, I'd originally hoped I would be one of those who got a placebo, but once I discovered they were for being nice, I changed my mind. Oh yes, and if we wish to, we can even take up the option of continuing with the drugs after the trials are finished – for free!

The tests were to start on Monday week, which was pretty much perfect. I was only employed at the school on a lesson-by-lesson, week-to-week basis, so I'd be able warn them of my unavailability for those two weeks – effectively a fortnight's holiday, but paid. Like I said, I'm really going to like this.

Ben

In the three weeks that passed after being kicked out of the agency, I hadn't done much, to be honest. Oh, I'd rung a few contacts, of course. But all I got back was stuff about recessions, downturns and cutbacks. And that's just the ones I could get through to. 'I'm sorry, I'm out of the office at present' became voicemail of the month.

You know, the non-working world is a slower, gentler place. You see different things, in different ways. For instance, when I was cooped up in an office all day I didn't see mums pushing babies, or little snakes of infant school children, or pensioners on buses, or huddles of smoking truants, or dog walkers or people just pausing and chatting. Come to think of it, I didn't even see daylight most of the fucking time! I hate the word irony, but as I sat on that park bench watching the real world go by, it did occur to me that I hadn't been seeing, I mean *really* seeing, any of the things that advertising people are supposed to know about.

Small parks are evocative places. You can sit and look back at your childhood: the toddler on the swings, with little gloved hands clasped tightly to the chains, pushed by his mum higher and higher, squealing with delight; the older kids, brave enough to stand up on the swing, heaving at its chains with feet forward and muscles clenched – heave and thrust until momentum is found, flying free; the same blissfulness that they might, if they're very lucky, experience in dreams when they become older. Then there's the little roundabout, forever squeaking at the same point in its cycle. Push it round faster and faster, picking up speed, clamber to the centre, turning and turning. Eyes closed, jump off as late as you dare. Stand there, head spinning. Head spinning? Unsteady? It's all Mum's fault. *That's* where I learnt how to do Fridays!

There, you see. Done it again. That last thought sort of sums me up. Just can't stay too serious, for too long. I have to make everything into a joke. Work, money, girls – jokes, footie, booze. Don't get too deep, Ben, you can't get drowned in the shallow end.

I let my eyes wander from the playground towards a group of older boys. They stood in a little group, smoking badly, gobbing well and feigning indifference toward a group of girls texting a short distance away.

You know, I consider myself young, but to them I'm not. When I was fifteen, a thirty-two-year-old was ancient. To them, I'm already a fucked old fart. Sitting here, unemployed and unwanted. I'm already mystified by half their music, amused by their clothes and disapproving of their behaviour. Hip, happening ad man. Yeah, right.

When you're unemployed you can spend hours watching this stuff, recalling your childhood, watching a new world replace the old. But unfortunately, in this particular new world, watching kids on the swings could also have you down as a nonce. So I moved on, wandering towards the park café.

I left school and started work as soon as it was legal. And had never regretted it, never looked back. Until now, perhaps. For the first time, I had doubts. But back then, when I first started out, it all seemed so simple. I got a job as a runner at a small ad agency, making tea and stuff. Then a year or so later, I found myself in the print department doing bits and pieces on Photoshop, and about a year on from that I got my big break. Almost overnight I became a Creative. How up your own arse does that sound eh: became a *Creative*? Anyway, the agency was pitching against some of the big boys for an anti-smoking campaign, but nobody was coming up with anything. I was a nobody, so maybe that's why it suddenly hit me. We could have posters that simply said: 'Smoking Is Good For You'. The public would wonder what the fuck was going on – how could the government put out ads like that? Then, two weeks later, we'd replace them with 'Smoking Is Good For You – *If* You're An Undertaker.' Later still, we'd add '*If* You're A Heart Surgeon', et cetera.

It wasn't my job to come up with ideas, but I emailed it to our Creative Director on spec and it just blew him away! He teamed me up with Ned, who was a Millwall-supporting colleague – only a junior himself, but at least he'd done the art school thing – and between us we perfected it. We followed this up with our 'Smoking Won't Kill You' campaign, which was a similar idea, adding: 'But The Cancer *Will*', and suddenly we were big shots! Twenty-five-year-old know-nothings from Sarf London: awards, gongs, piss-ups, you name it. Then we got poached by one of the big boys – the same big boy that's just given me the elbow, as it's turned out – and we came up with our 'Hire and Lower' campaign for their rental car account. More gongs, more backslapping, even posher piss-ups. The Cannes Advertising Festival, for example – charlie around pools, champagne on yachts and *wahay*!

After that we carried on the partying, but… well, we never quite hit those heights again. And the rest, as they say, is history.

So I had absolutely nothing on the horizon. Actually that's not true. Coming up were two weeks of lazing around and getting paid for doing fuck all. And if that sounds a bit like advertising, in this instance, it wasn't. You see, I'd taken Ned's advice and had volunteered for some clinical trials. I'd had a meeting with them, and a swift medical, a few days earlier. And apart from being a bit stressed out and having a few sleepless nights – I *had* just lost my bloody job, after all – surprisingly I was in pretty good shape. So they'd taken me. I had told a few porkies about the units though. Well, I'm a bloke, aren't I?

Actually, that was probably the main thing I was worrying about at the time. The only real drawback: two bloody weeks without substance abuse. That was going to be fun. Which was exactly why I was going out that very night for one last gigantic piss-up.

The Bull, Windsor One Day Before The Trials

'Sorry Amraj,' said Wyles, addressing his CSO whilst trying to attract the barman's attention. 'I still don't entirely get this whole faithfulness thing.'

'Why's that?' replied Amraj, standing just behind him.

'You know that fidelity stuff. What could possibly be the genetic advantage to being faithful – to *not* spreading your seed.'

A rather haughty looking woman, standing with her husband at the bar and holding a G&T, gave a disdainful look at the word 'seed'.

Oblivious to this and, with Wyles having now collared a barman, Amraj replied to the back of his boss's head: 'Ah yes, but it's not a male sex thing, it's a women sex thing.'

'Ah, right,' exhaled Wyles, turning around. 'I can well imagine.'

With drinks in hand – a beer for Wyles, a Coke for Amraj – they fought their way from the busy saloon bar and found a table.

'It's all down to some research that's been going on in America,' said Amraj, pulling up his chair. 'They've found that pheromones have an interesting effect on women on the pill. You see, during the trials, instead of fancying blokes who smell dissimilar to themselves – the way pheromones normally work – they suddenly reverted to fancying men who smelt *similar*. And the big question was obviously, why?'

'Obviously,' replied Wyles, sipping his pint and not certain what he was agreeing with.

'Well the reason is – the reason women appeared to break with recognized Darwinian logic…'

'Women break with *all* fucking logic, Amraj,' interrupted Wyles.

Amraj laughed, but continued: 'Seriously though, the reason why is that oral contraceptives trick women's bodies into thinking they're already pregnant. And pregnant women crave the familiarity of their home, of their own family, rather than going out to find new sexual partners. Put simply, we do seem to have chemicals in our bodies that keep us faithful – or at least, women do.'

'And that's the way our PC352 works?

'Pheroxosol,' corrected Amraj.

'Ah yes, Pheroxosol – that's the way it works?'

'Unintentionally, maybe – so we might find ourselves with an um, interesting set of results…'

'But surely we would be putting them into men *and* women.'

'Of course, yes. Both men and women need anti-depressants, don't they?'

'True,' agreed Wyles. He then thought for a second before adding: 'You know, even though officially we're developing some kind of nasal Prozac, I do think we should keep an eye on this whole other thing. I mean, if we *were* onto a sort of fidelity drug…'

They both sipped their drinks and, for a second, gave this some thought. However, they were thinking of entirely different things. Wyles, who had only recently had the time to consider its ramifications, rather liked what he was hearing, or perhaps smelling: money. Amraj, on the other hand, was lost in altogether more honorable considerations:

'I wonder whether it's entirely…'

'Entirely what?' asked Wyles, taking another swig.

'Well, whether it would be considered as a little… unethical?'

'Unethical! In what way?'

'Well, maybe not unethical as such, but we would be playing with people's emotions – you know, their whole lives.'

'Look Amraj,' replied Wyles, settling back again. 'We're making happy pills here. That's what they're *for*.'

'Yes, but just imagine if it *did* work as a...' Amraj leant back and thought for a second before continuing. 'Well, imagine if it *did* work as a sort of fall-in-love drug – after all, it wouldn't be the first drug to end up being used for something different – Viagra, for instance.'

'Exactly,' agreed Wyles.

'Imagine if we marketed Pheroxosol as an anti-depressant but it ends up being used as some kind of love stimulant?'

'I can't see why that's a problem,' shrugged Wyles. 'Could be a winner!'

'True, but would a drug like that – that affects people's *emotional* life – even be allowed?'

'Of course it would be fucking allowed. Most drugs affect people's emotional lives. Otherwise they wouldn't work.'

'Yes, but this would affect their... you know... the fundamentals of life – love, loyalty. I mean, if all that's down to a bunch of chemicals, what's it all about – being good, being bad, I mean?'

Wyles failed to answer that one – seemed more interested in the barmaid's tits – so Amraj just continued: 'You know, if just by pumping drugs into people we can change them into being nice, family people – well, it kind of brings everything into question, doesn't it?'

Wyles thought for a second. 'Okay, didn't you say something about using oxytocin to help mother's bond with babies?'

'Well, not as such, no. They use it to induce contractions – but it's reckoned that's a side effect, yes.'

'Well then, that's manipulating love and loyalty, isn't it – between mother and child – so where's the difference?'

'True,' shrugged Amraj.

'And anyway,' said Wyles, 'we don't seem to have a problem with pills for sex – for the physical side – do we?' Wyles was on a roll here – the tits had temporarily disappeared. So he just pressed on: 'I mean, think about it, what would the Victorians make of this bloody conversation?'

'How do you mean?'

'Well, we dole out drugs for endless erections, but not faithfulness – the thing that keeps families together. It tells us a lot about modern morals, doesn't it – a pill for sex is okay, but a pill for love is a no-no.'

He had a point, thought Amraj. 'A monogamy pill,' laughed Amraj, raising his glass. He then thought for a second and added: 'On the other hand, I mean, thinking about it, who would… '

'Buy it?'

'No, not that. Who would *control* it, *sell* it?

'Nation's favourite pushers,' said Wyles. 'The National Health Service.'

'They've got enough on their plate already. They're broke just trying to do all the other stuff.'

'Well I'm sure there'd be *some* government agency that'd go for it. After all, think about it: fewer STDs, fewer single parents, fewer domestics too probably – crime figures would plummet. Then there's housing.'

'*Housing?*'

'Yes. Fewer split-ups mean more houses.'

'Suppose so,' said Amraj, hardly able to keep up with his boss's opportunism.

'Then there's marriage guidance, of course. You know: counselors. All they do is *talk* people better. No money in that. About time they joined in.'

'Yes,' said Amraj, his head almost spinning. 'I suppose it is.'

'You see, Am, when it comes down to it, we caused this mess in the first place.'

'Mess?'

'Yes, people's lives. Us medical scientists, we've made people live longer. Now we need to do some work on marriage and stuff. It all needs to match up.'

Staggering home that night, Wyles found himself wondering whether he should give this Pheroxosol a go himself. After all, he did have some rather painful first-hand experience of failed relationships. There again, if it meant watching Iggle Piggle and the Ninky Nonk on a Friday night rather than the barmaid's knockers, perhaps not.

Lily

At ten-to-nine, prompt as ever, I pull my little wheely case into MediSee's reception. There's something about those little cases, especially when combined with a trouser suit – suggesting executive travel and expense accounts and stuff. None of which, I might add, I'd had the slightest experience of. But you have to play the part, don't you?

Beyond reception, the same kind-faced, though efficient, Angela Harty was there to say hello – ticking off my name, pointing me in the direction of a coffee-dispenser and a row of empty plastic seats. I wheeled my case to one of them – being first, as ever, there were plenty to choose from – parked it exactly in the middle of the row, got myself a hot chocolate and took it back to my seat.

It had taken me ages deciding what to put in that case. A good stock of non-transparent – though not too frumpy – underwear, jimjams, tee shirts, tracky bottoms and sloppy tops – all the kind of stuff they'd suggested we would need in the daytime. Luckily, they also had a laundry collection at the end of the first week, otherwise I'd have needed a truck. I also included all the obvious essentials: make-up, mirrors, brushes, nail scissors, hair dryers, toiletries – oh yes, and six books, three per week.

I'd had to consider all sorts of other issues too. Legs shaved, eyebrows plucked and fu-fu mercilessly mowed. Well, you never can tell when you're going to meet some gorgeous doctor, can you? Quite why a research doctor looking into depression would have his head between my legs, I couldn't say. But better to be safe than sorry, I thought.

I sat and waited. It was all quite exciting – a bit like going on holiday, really. Bit like being in a hospital waiting room, too.

After a few minutes, the first recruit arrived – or if you included me, the second. She was tall and slim and my immediate reaction was that if there was to be a doctor doing between-the-legs research, she would probably be first on his list. She checked in, walked over to me, put her hand out confidently and said: 'Hi, I'm Francine.'

I have a system with names. Well, as a TEFL teacher you really need one. You see, with mainstream teaching you have the same students for a term at the very least, whereas TEFL teachers have weekly changes, with names as effortlessly memorable as Ki Hyan and Xuan Thuy.

So, in Francine's case she had high cheekbones and an aquiline nose; in fact she was so Gallic looking that I could almost imagine her breathlessly whispering *je t'aime* whilst sipping a Pernod and puffing a Gitannes. As it turned out she came from Catford and spoke like Janet Street Porter, but that's neither here nor there. The point was that looks-wise Francine equalled France, which in turn equalled name remembered.

She'd just finished telling me how she works on an Elizabeth Arden counter in Bromley, and was only doing this for extra cash to get her foot on the property ladder, when the next recruit arrived. He introduced himself as Russell. Now, rustle is the sound that autumn leaves make and that was the colour of his hair – easy. By the time he'd told us how he'd only just graduated from Newcastle – studying irrigation, or something – a steady flow was arriving. A Chris came over and said hello. I couldn't think of any characteristics I could associate with his name so I just had to use old-fashioned memory. A guy called Tim, who was probably gay, also said hello. He was easy. On the name front, that is. He had a little quiffy bit on the top of his head like the cartoon character Tin Tin. So Tin Tin sounded like Tim, which equated to name remembered. A John introduced himself – this is just like a party, I thought – he was quite good looking and had those thick, black, horn rimmed spectacles that Johnny Depp looks his sexiest in. So Johnny equalled John, equalled name remembered. Another post grad, this time called Claudia said hi. She seemed vague and cloudy, so that was easy. And a slightly older guy called Josh was next. He had a sort of crumpled faced with squashed features. Josh sounds like squash, so, hopefully, name remembered.

There seemed to be a split between those who were doing all the meeting and greeting, and those who took seats and kept to themselves. As the less sociable ones seemed to have resigned, slightly bored looks on their faces, I took them to be clinical veterans who had probably seen it all before; us jabberers, on the other hand, were using up all our nervous energy – all a bit like a *Big Brother* first night.

After about twenty minutes Angela Harty rejoined us, so presumably we were all present and correct. I looked around. There were about twenty of us, give or take, with a roughly equal male-female split. At a guess we were all somewhere in between our mid-twenties and, in the case of Josh, late thirties.

'Hi everyone,' she said.

'Hi,' we all replied.

She ran through a short welcoming speech and then asked us to follow her. Francine and I were almost at the back so we couldn't see much, though Angela's stewardess-style to-the-left and to-the-right hand signals – pointing out toilets, dining areas and corridors – did help.

The layout seemed pretty much as I had remembered it from the interview, but I think the tour was as much about team bonding as finding your way around – with Nurse Angela trotting out a few well worn jokes about bottles of whisky in bedside cabinets and bed hopping during the night – getting a few ripples of laughter in response.

We were in the day room, with Angela telling us all about the dining area, the Sky, the broadband and even the games compendium – Scrabble and all – when from just behind us came a cough, followed by a croaked out: 'Um, 's'cuse me.'

Being at the back of the group when we turned, I was nearest to him.

A term my mum used to use came immediately to mind. It was something she used to say when my big sister and I came back from playing in the park on long, hot summer days. Through a hedge backwards. And that's exactly what he looked like. I say 'he' because I think it was male. But not necessarily human male. It was sopping wet, unshaven, scraggly-haired and grey faced – with bloodshot eyes. He (yes, it was definitely human) was wearing a smelly tee shirt, filthy jeans and grimy, flapping sneakers. And absolutely stank of stale booze.

There was a brief silence. We all looked at him.

'Sorry I'm late,' he said.

As in dead, I thought.

'Aha, Mr Dryden, I presume,' said Angela, making her way through the group. She looked at him and then said: 'I think you should go back to the reception, don't you? I'll see you when I'm finished.'

Using my system on mnemonics, only one name comes to mind for this idiot. However, I very much doubt that his mother christened him Numpty.

Ben

I had made up my mind to be a nicer, more well-rounded person. I had made up my mind to be healthier too. Then there was the money thing. I was never, for instance, going to get drunk on stupidly priced club booze. I was never going to try to impress some girl I'd never see again by buying her a bottle of even more stupidly priced champagne. I was never going to fill a table with food I was too pissed to eat. I was never going to insist, to the point of almost throwing punches, that I should cover the cost of a cab home with Ned. And I was never again going to get up so late that I needed a black cab.

Stop, go, lurch, start, stop. And all the time the automatic door-locking thingy's clicking on and off. And all the time the meter's ticking money. And all the time the driver's talking bollocks.

I was on the verge of retching as I stumbled from that taxi into the pouring London rain. He had dropped me right outside the hospital, in an unfamiliar street. I staggered to the main entrance and found my way to a likely looking desk.

You know, it says a lot about the way you look when, arriving at hospital's enquiry point, the bloke behind the glass says: 'A&E's that way, mate.'

'No,' I panted, with rain and sweat streaking my face. 'I want that research place, where they do tests and stuff.'

'Do you mean MediSee?'

'Yes, yes, that's it.'

He told me to go back the way I came, turn right, then go to the next building and then it's first on the right.

I did as I was told, stumbling and swerving my way past oncoming medics. I crashed out through the double doors and, with rain cascading down from the guttering above, pulled my jacket over my head and hunched along as near to the wall as I could. I somehow missed the turning completely, found myself in a puddle-filled ambulance park, ran back, found the turning and eventually, absolutely drenched, found MediSee's main doors.

I all but fell into the reception and stood there, wiping water from my clothes, face and hair. Then I realized it was completely empty. There was absolutely no one around. So I stood there for a few seconds, dripping onto the floor tiles.

Shit! My bag! The taxi!

Already an hour late, taxi long gone – there was nothing I could do.

From somewhere in the building I heard laughter. I followed the sound, past a row of empty chairs, down a corridor and through an empty common room. Then, to my right and through glazed swing doors, I saw the source. A group of people in jackets and coats were listening to, as far as I could see, the nurse who had originally interviewed me. At least I think it was her.

I pushed through the door, coughed and said something – you know, to get their attention. The whole group turned to look at me. One of the people nearest me, a girl, gave me a look that suggested I was some kind of bacterial infection.

Then it all went very quiet.

'Yes?' said the nurse, breaking the silence and pushing her way to the front.

I couldn't think what to say.

She was standing right in front of me. 'Ben Dryden, I presume.'

I said nothing.

'I think you should go back to the reception, don't you? I'll see you when I'm finished.'

I trudged back, feeling a prat. Back at school again.

I took a plastic seat, leant forward and put my head in my hands. The nausea came in waves, and again, I felt like vomiting – but didn't. So I leant back, but felt no better, and waited for perhaps fifteen more minutes.

Finally, as I was about to nod off, she appeared. 'Mr Dryden,' she commanded, as I cleared my eyes, 'this is Dr Taylor.'

Next to her was a man in a white coat. He looked down at me over the top of his wire-rimmed glasses.

'Hi,' I said.

'Hello,' he replied. 'Perhaps we should go to my office.'

This was beginning to feel familiar. Whatever you do, Ben, don't sing *Blue Moon*.

I got up, followed them. After a short walk he ushered me into a small, bright room.

'Take a seat,' he said, continuing around to the far side of his desk. I took a seat. The nurse also came in, positioning herself to his left. Yes, I've been here before. Football manager's line: '*Déjà vu, all over again.*'

It was all very light and airy. Office-wise, nothing like I was used to. White coats, gleaming surfaces – like a toothpaste ad, in fact. I was the only dirty thing there. Frankly, I thought, if I'm going to be bollocked, I'd rather it was in a dungeon. When you're feeling shit, you want to *be* in shit.

'Well firstly, Ben. You're an hour late,' said the nurse.

Now that's not nice either. I mean, you expect to be questioned by the person dead opposite you – looking directly into your eyes. Not by someone off to the side. I turned my attention to her, just as Dr Taylor chimed in with: 'But that's not the main problem.' Here we go again. I thought I was here for drug trials, not a fucking PowerPoint pitch.

'Look,' I said, 'I'm sorry I'm late, but I left my case in a cab.'

'Okay,' he said, giving an understanding nod. 'But like I said, that's not the main problem.'

I remained silent.

'You are aware, Ben, of the rules relating to alcohol in these trials?'

I waited for a second and considered his question. Of course I bloody was. That's why I'd been out on the piss. 'Yes,' I finally replied.

'So if you don't mind my asking,' he enquired, looking over his glasses. 'Are you hungover?'

Ah, so that's it. That's what all the fuss is about.

'Well yes, I suppose I am,' I shrugged. 'I had a few drinks last night.'

I didn't actually add 'So fucking what!', but I might just as well have done.

'A few?' he questioned.

I didn't answer that. To me, it's a few.

'Look,' he continued, 'the efficacy of this drug could be affected by alcohol – most drugs are – and depending on the amount of alcohol you've got in your bloodstream, we may not be able to start your course today. Now frankly, if that's the case, you might as well go home.'

After a deep breath, I looked down at my fingers. 'I see,' I said.

And I could. I could exactly see.

'So you lost your case?' he asked, changing the subject.

Actually, I'd completely forgotten my case.

'Yes,' I said, looking very sorry for myself. 'I left it in a cab – when I got out, I mean – at the hospital's reception.'

'Angela will take you to the ward,' he said, sort of kindly. 'We'll make some enquiries for you.'

Lily

The first day went pretty smoothly. It was rainy and windswept when I arrived, so the thought of getting paid to lounge about in centrally heated, all-mod-con surroundings was fine by me.

Soon after I'd folded my clothes, lined up my toiletries, changed out of my posh clobber and settled into my room, the doctor arrived. He was anything but hunky, being middle-aged and unremarkable, but in a way that was comforting – peering over his spectacles and looking the part. He asked me a few questions, took my blood pressure and listened to my heart. Literally, that is. Dr Taylor was his name.

I did suffer a tiny bit of stage fright in the what-to-wear front before going into the day room. It was fine dressing up in a power suit for the journey, but this was where real life kicked in, or real life for the next couple of weeks, anyway.

I plumped for tracky bottoms and a sloppy top. It was difficult really because on the one hand that was the kind of stuff they'd recommended – and it did make loads of sense – but on the other, that was the kind of person you'd see slopping around on some sink estate. If I'm sounding a bit snobby about this it's because I probably am. Upbringing, you see. *Guardian*-reading, liberal and tolerant. Therefore intolerant. Sell my body for science, yes. Wear a onesie, absolutely not.

I even had trouble in deciding which book to take down on my first day, but in the end, because I felt sort of holiday-ish – not too posh – I went for a David Nicholls. And on that subject, saying I'm taking it *down* with me says a lot. After all, it was all on the same floor. But somehow it felt as though I was going down to a beach or a pool or something. Bit sad, really.

As I stood in front of the mirror and picked off the last few bits of dust from my terry top, I did have one last thought. I bet the blokes wouldn't be going through this hell. I bet they wouldn't be spending forty minutes agonizing over what to wear for a grand entry into a hospital corridor (especially having already spent three days doing it at home). Oh well, *vive le indifference!*

Instantly, I found myself wondering why I'd bothered. With all agonizing, I mean. The first thing I saw, in fact the only thing I saw, when I walked into the dayroom, was three scruffy blokes, lounging all over the sofas, watching football and not even giving me a second look. Hardly worth the effort.

'Hi,' I said to the backs of three heads.

'Hi,' said two of them – Josh and Chris, I think – without even turning.

The third was definitely Russell, but it hardly mattered because, apart from a slight turn of the head, his only other response was to scratch his balls through his tracksuit bottoms. Nice.

Nothing changes, does it? Boyfriends, husbands, brothers, sons. Married *to* them, divorced *from* them, mother*ing* them. Blokes I'd known for years, blokes I hadn't. But all just standard issue, 'doesn't do what it says on the man' men. I might as well have not existed.

So I moved away from the TV and scrotum-scratching department, sat down and opened my book. I couldn't really get started, so I picked up an old copy of *Marie Claire* and flipped through it.

After a few minutes Francine turned up. Now she *had* tried. I thought the whole point of these all-in-one things was that they were supposed to be casual and sort of sloppy. Not hers. Okay, like mine it was made of comfortable material, but that's where the similarity ended. Champagne-coloured, it hugged her like a coat of paint – an *under*coat of paint. It also had a zip that went from neck to navel and a rather suggestive ring-pull.

And pulled it had been – to a point far nearer the navel than the neck.

Now what was I saying about blokes? Suddenly, football didn't matter. It was all 'Hi Francine' this and 'How are you, Francine?' that. And even 'Would you like another channel, Francine?' Another channel! Because she's got her tits half out! Perhaps if I got mine *completely* out they'd turn the fucking footie off! Then again, perhaps they wouldn't.

She was obviously accustomed to such attention though and, taking the whole thing in stride, said a brief hello to them and continued over to me. She then asked if she could join me (remembering my name in the process), sat down next to me and, just as before, was pretty normal. Okay, she may have had a WAG's figure and an Eastender's accent, but, plunging neckline apart (and I may perhaps have exaggerated that a little), came across as very pleasant.

Somewhere down the line a bit of late breakfast must have been laid on because some of the guys were watching TV with bowls of cereal in their hands (thanks fellas!). So Francine and I went to the dining area and found some muesli and toast and stuff – all very hotel like – and sat down at one of the two big tables. We jawed away about one thing and another and then topped up our coffees and took them back to the common room sofas. Very soon we were joined by Claudia, who was as vague and dreamy as before, plus two other girls, Vicky and Jasmine, whom I hadn't previously met.

Once we got past where we lived and what we did (Vicky and Jasmine were students), we spoke of likes and dislikes and family and stuff. All very normal. Then a girl called Sophie turned up who, like Francine, was another real looker. They were completely different though. Whereas Francine had long auburn hair, Sophie's was black and cropped, and whereas Francine was languid and sultry, Sophie was sparkling and lively.

Perhaps the only subject we didn't really get round to was blokes, but I wouldn't imagine that either of them had too many troubles in that department. Or, put another way, perhaps they had loads.

And talking of blokes, the first male to wander over to our group was John-with-the-glasses, followed by probably-gay-Tim. Then, about an hour later, two more boys turned up, both ex-grads, called Brendan and Dom. And decent though they were (Brendan dark and broody, Dom tousled and boyish) they were perhaps a bit young for me. And then it occurred to me. Something I should have admitted to myself a long time ago. I was not only treating this whole exercise as a nice little earner, but as a dating opportunity. And that, deep down, was why I'd spent so much time in front of the mirror and why I was so intensely sizing up the likes of Francine and Sophie.

Soon after Brendan and Dom turned up, Nurse Angela came in and we all stopped jabbering. She told us that food would soon be served (we had already guessed that from the aroma) and that it would be at this time everyday. She also said that Dr Taylor had asked her to pass on one further piece of information about the medication – being that it would be unlikely to have any effect for a couple of days: 'So don't necessarily expect to go out like a light tonight, or anything.' She then signed off with: 'That's not to say I'm expecting Glastonbury either!' This got the customary ripple of laughter, after which we all moved across to two large tables in the dining area.

I found myself sitting between Francine and Sophie. Now that's another interesting thing. Not the fact that I'd found myself stuck between the two most beautiful girls in the group but a wider observation about seating arrangements that I'd found as a TEFL teacher.

You see, you regularly get new groups of students who've never previously met each other, but will then spend perhaps the next two months together in the same classroom. And I can guarantee that the people they sit down next to on day one will be roughly the same people they'll sit down next to for the duration. I don't know why that is, but, except in rare circumstances, it's what happens. Oh well, at least I could pretend it was me the boys were ogling.

By now we were all beginning to get on more familiar terms with each other and I noticed that Francine had taken to calling John and Russell, who were sitting dead opposite us, Johnny and Russ. I suppose that's a confidence thing too. Being happy to drop so easily into such familiarities, I mean. Neither of the boys seemed to mind this (well, they wouldn't, would they?) but with John-with-the-glasses now mutated to Johnny, he had an even more Depp-like quality to him. In turn, Russell (sorry, Russ) had started referring to Sophie as Sophe, so it was all getting pretty cosy.

Food-wise we all queued at the trolleys and came back with our preferred nosh. There was a choice between fish pie and bangers and mash, neither of which I went for and the vegetarian lasagna, which I did.

It was then, whilst we were tucking into our main course, that one final member of our team arrived. It was Hedge Backwards Numpty. He loped in, appraised the landscape, went back to the food trolleys, slouched back with a plate brimming over with food and found himself a seat at the far end of the table, between Chris and Vicky. I think he mumbled something to Chris, possibly asking if the chair was free. That apart though, he said nothing – just put his head down and ate.

Johnny whispered his name to us. Apparently it was Ben. He only knew this because he'd briefly met him when he'd been back to the ward for something.

I couldn't think of anything that would work using my patented memory system. Looks-wise, perhaps Rhys Ifans in Notting Hill would be most similar. But his name was Spike.

Oh well, I wouldn't need to remember his name anyway. Way too nonchalant and full of himself for my liking. Hadn't even bothered to introduce himself. In fact, hadn't said anything. No, certainly not my type. Quite a contortionist too. After all, not only was he through a hedge backwards – he was up his own arse at the same time.

Ben

I was shown to a bed in a ward and crashed out onto it, or into it, or whatever, and fell asleep.

I had this dream. I don't normally remember my dreams, but I do remember this one. I think it was all related to everything I'd been through. Tiny, my ex boss, was in it – grown even fatter, like some huge, perspiring hippo. So was the doctor, I think: as a white coated Gestapo. They put me in this room, a bit like a ward, but with only one bed in it. They blindfolded me and said I'd have to come up with a good reason why I'd fucked up. Otherwise I'd be shot. It was horrible. I think it was connected to a movie I'd seen. School was somewhere in there too – in fact it could have been my teacher rather than Tiny. I was crap at lessons. Good at football, though.

Also in the dream, hanging over me, was a need to come up with an answer. But they didn't say what the question was. I suppose it was to do with presentations and stuff – or to do with exams. Same terror. Recently, I'd been experiencing a new version. Before picking up the phone and hustling for work. The same fear. Rejection. And then, when people told you there was nothing going, the pretending. Laughing it off. The chirpy 'see you soons', the telephone high-fives: 'That's okay, mate. No worries.'

I think my dad was in there too, though God knows why. Hardly knew him.

I must have woken, or partially woken, and lay there feeling rough. Somehow, the whole hospital thing was turning into prison. I was there because I'd fucked up. Two weeks inside.

Assuming they wanted me, that is. No partying, no friends, no nothing. God, I wouldn't have been doing this if I hadn't been such a twat. The agency ski trip was coming up. I could have done the whole snowboarding thing. Or maybe I'd have been on a shoot somewhere nice and warm. A location in Caribbean, maybe. You only have to start your script with something like '*Open on a palm-fringed beach*' and you're off. Actually, '*Open on a Croydon supermarket*' would have done me. Anything but this fucking place. On consideration, if this medical lot didn't want me, that's fine. *No one likes us, we don't care.*

After a while some bloke with glasses turned up. In fact, it could've been him that woke me. He seemed to have the bed next to mine and was looking in the drawers of his cabinet or something. He introduced himself, but I can't remember his name. I'm shit with names. Then I opened my eyes properly, yawned and sat up.

My case was there! Next to my bed! Excellent! They must have got it back. Result!

Whoever the bloke with the glasses was, he'd left the ward. Alone again. I unzipped my case, found my toilet bag and found the showers.

Boy did it feel good. I dried myself, slowly dressed in some clean clothes and even more slowly made my way to where I could hear voices.

There were maybe fifteen, sixteen people there. Sitting at two tables. They were all eating away and chattering, so I found the plates and cutlery, moved along to the food, piled on some sausages, a load of mash and some gravy, found an empty seat and sat down. About 50/50 blokes to girls, I'd say. A few decent ones too. Women, I mean. Not at my end of the table though, so I never got to speak to them. There was this one with long, chestnut hair. Great tits too. And one with short black hair and big eyes. There was another girl too. Between them. She caught my eye, or perhaps I caught hers. Gave me a look. Silly tart. Just because I was scraping my plate clean. Who the fuck did she think she was?

It brought back to me something Ned said once. The Disapprovers, he calls them. Women. Sort of negative superheroes who have the ability to instantly transform happy situations into complete shit. In Ned's opinion, sometimes it can happen within minutes of meeting them. That's why it's best just to move on. Then again, this wasn't exactly a happy situation in the first place.

According to the bloke on my left – I can't remember his name, like I said I'm crap with names – we were all supposed to go back to the ward. I told him I wasn't sure if I was included, but did anyway.

Soon afterwards, I was sitting back on my bed, and the doctor came in. Perhaps he saw me first because he had more to tell me – filled me in with all the stuff he said he'd told the others. I can't remember most of it. I'm crap with details too. He warned me that the drugs wouldn't have much effect at first, especially in my case. The night before and all. Oh yes, and it's nasal.

Funny, I used the wrong word. 'So you snort it?' I said.

'It's *inhale*, Ben,' he replied.

Later, I got to talk to some of the blokes in the ward. I found out who did what, but instantly forgot. Most were grads and gap years, and I felt a little bit out of my depth, to be honest. The word inadequate came to mind – not a word I'd previously have used about myself. That whole shallow end thing, I suppose. Oh well, at least they weren't married or had kids, so I felt slightly more comfortable with that. Committed generation, eh! Oh yes, and I did ask them which teams they supported but they said things like Man U and Chelsea, which means none at all.

At about six o'clock it began to dawn on me. I kind of knew it was going to come, but I hadn't really expected it that early – what with the previous night's piss-up, I mean. A drink. I could have killed for one.

I'm not an alcoholic or anything. I can live without it. It's just that at that particular point I could really have done with one. And thinking about it, I couldn't think of the last time I'd had a completely dry day.

You know, since I started telling you this story, it's the second time that I've said that: '*I'm not an alcoholic.*' And the first time I was lying unconscious on a bench outside a tube station. This time I'm in a hospital ward.

Doesn't sound great, does it?

Lily

Over the next couple of days we fell into some sort of routine. The mornings consisted of medication and tests (blood and urine) in our rooms, followed by breakfast and chit-chat in the eating area. This was followed by reading, more chatting (mainly girls), video games and TV (mainly boys) in the dayroom. Then more medication and more tests (urine and saliva), after which lunch was served. The food was good and solid – fish, meat and veggie options –if anything, given that we weren't allowed to leave the place, one of the main problems could have been weight gain. There was an exercise bike but it was enclosed in a small and rather sweaty room so I didn't fancy it – especially as a couple of the boys did. The last thing I needed was half an hour of sweaty-saddled, armpit-smelling confinement.

The afternoons had slightly more variance, not so much on the drugs, tests and gossip front, but on activities. We had a couple of extended games of Monopoly, with me always ending up in a squat in The Old Kent Road and Johnny, Russ, Sophie and Jasmine ending up with Paris Hilton-sized hotel empires. And we even had some live entertainment because Josh, who unbeknown to all had brought along his guitar, was a bit of a troubadour on the quiet.

He was a shy type, I suppose musicians often are, and it all started with him just strumming quietly in the corner. We soon found out though – on the occasions when he'd pause with plectrum still poised, quietly answering between chords – that he'd done studio work. He was also an occasional busker – and not half bad. I could well imagine him lazily propping up a wall in some windy underground walkway, knocking out Bob Dylans or David Greys.

Mind you, he could cover more than that, and had a pretty diverse repertoire. He even did a little Ronan Keating medley for me: '*Life Is A Rollercoaster*' and '*When You Say Nothing At All*' – which brought back memories of my long lost teens. And after I'd told him a little bit about my university years, he even devoted a song to me – from Adam. It almost brought me to tears. Oh yes and one night, for a laugh and having done some rock anthems for the boys, he even did a few girlie numbers: '*It's Raining Men*' and '*I Will Survive*'. Not that we danced or anything. I don't think we were really the 'dance around the handbag with Bacardi Breezer' types. But we did all sing along.

So did I fancy Josh? Well, he certainly wasn't what you'd call handsome. On the other hand, his crumpled, world-weary features did sort of come alive when he was singing out a particularly agonizing line. And anyway, looks aren't everything are they. And we did seem to get on. On the Tuesday morning we'd been first down for breakfast and got talking; not about anything in particular, just work and family and things, and we sort of clicked.

But no, not Josh. You see, he was easily the oldest of us, possibly forty, and I reckon he had some baggage tucked away somewhere. Those lived-in features, that old guitar. Anyway, I don't think he was that interested in me; in a romantic sense, I mean. We were just two people thrown together by coffee, cereal and one of his favourite strumalongs: *It ain't me babe… it ain't me you're looking for, babe.*

What of the others? Well the two grads, Brendan and Dom, were freshmen in all senses of the word. Cheeky and cherubic respectively, in some ways they would have made perfect partners. For a girl born ten years later, that is. Not so much that they were too young for me, more me too old for them. Too grumpy, especially in the morning. I couldn't deal with all that youth and beauty first thing.

Then there was Johnny and Russ, two guys who I'd spent more time with than any of the others. They would have been just perfect (individually, of course), being both good looking and good company. But the reason they were my main (male) company was because Francine and Sophe were my main (female) company. It was becoming increasingly obvious that Johnny had designs on Francine and Russ was eyeing up Sophie. And I can't say I blamed them. They were easily the best looking girls amongst us. And anyway, I don't want to sound too random. I don't go around dropping everything (metaphorically) for just anything. Which brings us to Tim, who was gay, and Chris, who was so quiet he was invisible. And that idiot, Ben.

The incident that summed Ben up was my first main encounter with him. I say first *main* encounter, but obviously there'd been the episode at our induction; stumbling in an hour late like some kind of alcoholic daddy-long-legs. No, what I mean is the first time I actually *spoke* to him. If you could call it that.

I've got this theory about his sort of behaviour and it's all tied up with the remembering people's names and stuff. You'll find you *do* remember people like Ben. You might not want to, but you do. Their stupidity makes them impossible to forget, so they stick out from the crowd. And I think that's why they do it. Attention seeking. Well that's my opinion, anyway.

So back to this incident. It was almost lights out time and I was lying in my bed reading my book and on the verge of nodding off. Then I heard this crash in the corridor – like a tray being dropped or something. Of course, that woke me up like a shot. A few seconds later, there was some silly male giggling and some loud *shhh, shhh, shhhhs* like someone trying, not very successfully, to be quiet.

I got up, put on my dressing gown, crept to the door and put my head round. Standing a few feet down the corridor was Chris – quiet Chris – looking a little sheepish and holding what would appear to be a football made of sticky tape and paper.

I then looked down at my feet. Staring at the ceiling, spread-eagled, looking like some incapacitated stick insect: Ben.

'What do you think you're doing?' I asked.

'Foul!' shouted Ben, before breaking into an uncontrollable fit of giggles.

'We agree on one thing, then,' I replied, before turning round and slamming the door.

Idiot.

I just lay there, unable to sleep, just thinking. Perhaps I'm a bit harsh sometimes, a bit of a killjoy. I don't always join in with other people, don't really let my hair down. Not that for one minute I'd like play silly football with that oaf, but you know what I mean. I've always been a bit solitary.

Okay, it is good to be comfortable with your own company, but I'm perhaps a bit too bookish sometimes.

I made up my mind to give Suzie a ring the next day. We were allowed visitors and I did promise her I'd give her a bell once I was all settled in. Oh yes and my sister, Jen, too. She might even bring little Thomas along.

Ben

I was sitting up in my hospital bed at about ten-thirty in the morning, all the others had gone for breakfast or whatever – wondering whether to get up.

'Mooornin',' I heard.

I looked up. Completely unannounced, it was Ned!

'Lucozade!' he said, pulling out a bottle and sitting down on my bed.

'Thanks mate, good to see you.' I nodded at the bottle and said: 'But er, I'm not ill.'

'Okay,' he said, snatching it back. 'I took some to Nan when *she* was in hospital – *and* Granddad.' He then thought for a second and added, 'There again, they both snuffed it… so… on second thoughts.'

He put the bottle back on my bedside cabinet.

'Thanks, a bundle,' I said. 'Either way, I don't think I'm allowed it.'

'How about grapes, then?' he said, fishing out a brown crumpled bag.

'Don't think I'm allowed them either.'

'Ungrateful sod.'

'Un-*grape*-ful?' I suggested, laughing.

'That's awful,' he replied, shaking his head and taking a handful.

Nothing had changed really. We were still a team, could still come up with one-liners, ideas. It was just that, sadly, his half of the team was still working in advertising and my half wasn't.

He leant forward conspiratorially, winked, nodded towards the bottle and said: 'Actually, it's not Lucozade – it's er, for the long, lonely nights.'

He meant well, but I shook my head. 'It's a lovely thought, Ned, but I can't. Booze is totally banned.'

'Exactly. That's why I put voddy in it.'

'Sorry Ned, the last time I looked, vodka was most definitely alcohol.'

'Yes but it doesn't *smell* like it does it. They'll never know. Unless you down the whole fucking lot in one, of course.'

'No Ned, I think you're missing the point.' I adjusted my pillow and pulled myself up in the bed a little. 'You see, it's not a case of *pretending* not to drink, I'm actually *not drinking*.'

'Sorry?'

'I said I'm not drinking.'

'For two weeks! You? You're having a giraffe!'

I had already made up my mind that I was going to toe the line on this one and, so far, it had been easier than I thought it would be. Of course, being in a hospital was the perfect place to be on the wagon. A bit like rehab, I suppose. I certainly couldn't guarantee I'd have been as self-disciplined out on the streets. So I was determined to stick with it while I was in the hospital, at least.

'Lucozade, grapes, voddy,' he shrugged. 'Your loss, my gain.' He stuffed the bottle back into his bag with his other gifts.

Of course, his feelings weren't genuinely hurt. It was all a bit of nonsense; one of those little games we played. We could refuse presents, forget presents, rib each other – physically assault each other – but somehow, it never caused real offence. From what I've seen, it doesn't work like that with girls. Okay, they might be more supportive, especially with love and stuff – they're miles better with relationships and heartbreaks and life's big problems. They also share more *and* give more time – long, in-depth discussions; Facebook, phone calls and millions of photo attachments on their emails. One wedding can crash an entire office block. But if their best mate says just one thing out of line, that's it.

Back at the agency there was a girl called Philipa. She worked just down the corridor in Account Management. Her best friend was a girl called Emily, from Media Buying. Inseparable, they were. They did everything together – well, not everything, but you know what I mean. Apparently, one day, Philipa said something that suggested – only suggested, mind – that Emily's trousers weren't great. They were still okay, they were still passable, but they weren't great. Worse than that, they weren't new either – Emily had worn them many times before. Now that's also illogical. After all, I'd be more pissed off if they were new. An old pair being shit is no problem. They don't owe you anything, so you just throw them away. But that's not the way women's minds work. Or Emily's anyway. The idea that she'd been wearing something for six months that made her arse look a little plump (I believe that was the problem) was catastrophic. Apparently, in the female world, it would have been preferable for poor Philipa to have said, many months earlier: 'By the way, Emily, your arse looks huge.' But she didn't. She merely informed her, six months down the line, that they probably weren't the best trousers in her wardrobe. So we had an afternoon of tears, a week of silence, two months of brooding and the end of life-long friendship.

Ned only stayed at the clinic for an hour or so, but that was fine – like I said, blokes aren't as generous with their time as girls. We went down to the dayroom, had a coffee, met some of the others and played a couple of games of *Destroy All Humans: The Path Of Furon*.

Just after that – just as he was leaving, in fact – he told me had a new partner. Copywriting partner, that is. I suppose I shouldn't have been upset. After all, he needed a partner, didn't he? You don't get teams of one, do you? So I should have been fine with it. But I wasn't. In fact, I felt rejected, and when I found out who his partner was – some public school twerp called Jay – I felt even worse.

Then a strange (and for me, alien) thought occurred to me. I suddenly realized how immature I was being; how ridiculous I was. I mean, doesn't it say a lot about advertising, and a lot about me? The only time I feel jealous, the only time I feel snubbed, is when my workmate, not *girlfriend*, but *workmate*, finds a new partner. How sad is that? But like I said, that wasn't typical of me. Relationships hadn't been my thing. Up until then, anyway.

After Ned left, not much else happened. Just the normal stuff: some lunch and some dinner and some boring old TV. Oh yes and I hurt my arm. Not badly though; it was just before lights out. Chris and Russ were playing footie when I happened to be walking down the same corridor that they were using as a goal. Russ kicked the ball – actually, it wasn't a proper ball, just a ball of paper – and I trapped it. Russ then came barging into me and I went flying – arse over tit – hitting a trolley as I fell.

I could see the funny side – or perhaps, not so much the funny side, as the funny bone, because that's what I hit and that's why I sort of laughed. It's an odd sensation, not really funny at all. Oh yes, and I pissed off that Lily girl in the process – that one that keeps giving me odd looks. I suppose I woke her up. She poked her head round the door. God knows what she thought of me, lying there giggling. But it wasn't too bad. She soon went back to where she came from. And truthfully, it's only because of what happened as a result of this event that I even remember it now. Seminal moment.

The Coach & Horses, Eton

The distance between the outer edges of Slough, where CalmerCeutical's laboratory lies, and the village of Eton, is about two miles. Yet the gap between the two is the whole world. Slough, famously unloved but incredibly productive, is a town of factories, office blocks and industrial estates. Eton, educationally renowned but irritatingly cute, is a town of tea shops, boaters and picnics on the river.

Now if, like William Wyles, you're a boss with a generous expense account, given the choice between a fast food outlet in a run-down high street and a picturesque pub in an idyllic riverside setting, it's no choice at all. And that's why he made that short journey once a week.

His hostelry of choice was the Coach & Horses, an impossibly pretty little pub with views from its mullioned windows of Windsor Castle serenely reflected on the sleepy river Thames.

And about once a month, assuming their busy schedule allowed – and somehow it always did – he also entertained the senior members of his management team there.

They'd all turn up in their cars – none of them as big and beastly as Wyles's – order their pints of Brakspears from the bar, find their regular table and, rubbing their hands in anticipation, order steaks and puddings, settle back and natter – kicking off, as ever, on non-work issues:

'Weather's looking up,' remarked Tom Delaney, the Financial Director, nodding towards the sunny windows.

'Yeah,' agreed Martin Samuel of Corporate Strategy. 'Be able to get a bit of golf in soon.'

'Ah yes, that reminds me,' said Wyles, CEO. 'Must sort out that trip.'

This was something he'd promised them all once the whole Pheroxosol thing was put to bed. 'I was thinking of April. The greens should be pretty good down there by then,' he added, referring to the Algarve.

'Certainly should be,' agreed Theo Hoskins, General Manager, who lost no opportunity in reminding everyone that he had a place there.

They spent the next twenty minutes discussing handicaps and holidays until the food arrived, when Tom Delaney brought the subject back to Pheroxosol: 'So what's all this stuff about it being some kind of *luurve* brew, Amraj?' he smirked, unfurling his napkin.

Of all the executives present, Amraj, being neither a drinker nor a socializer, was probably the least comfortable in such surroundings. But when the conversation turned back to lab work, even if flippantly, he was always happy to join in. 'It was just a thought, really,' he shrugged adding: 'I honestly don't think it's very likely.'

'Tell you what,' said Wyles to his marketing man, 'it'd be an interesting sales exercise, wouldn't it?'

'Certainly would be,' agreed Samuel.

They all then spent time coming up with rather unlikely and, in some cases, downright crude ideas for marketing such a drug, before Samuel said: 'Tell you what fellas, how about: *Pheroxosol: You'll Fall In Love With It.*'

'Very good,' enthused Wyles. 'Must remember that one.'

'Seriously though,' countered Amraj, 'we'll probably never know anyway, these tests aren't designed for that.'

That kind of stifled the conversation for a bit, and they all got down to some serious eating. Then Wyles wiped his mouth with his napkin and observed: 'Now here's an interesting thought.'

'What's that, Will?' asked Amraj.

'Well, how would you even design clinical trials around love? I mean it's pretty difficult to calculate, isn't it?'

'Totally,' agreed Amraj. 'And, apart from anything else, it would depend on who you got for the tests. I mean, before the whole love thing kicks in you *do* need to fancy someone, don't you?'

'Not necessarily,' joked Hoskins. 'Some people – not a million miles from here – would shag anything with or *without* a pulse.'

'I assume that was aimed at me,' remarked Samuel, the only single man amongst them.

'If the cap fits,' laughed Wyles.

This little distraction seemed to go right over Amraj's head and he continued with the conjecture: 'Scientifically speaking, it would be really difficult because if, for instance, the drug was working on one person, but not on another, results-wise you'd still end up with a big fat zero.'

'I see your point,' concurred Wyles. 'It takes two to tango.'

'Precisely.'

'So how *would* you profile them?' asked Hoskins, as he forked a piece of sausage into his mouth.

'What, the recruits?' asked Amraj.

'Yeah.'

'Couples with problems, maybe,' he shrugged. 'Then you could see how their relationship changes.'

'Yes, but they don't come with a clean slate, do they?'

'True,' agreed Amraj. 'Frankly, it's not really my area. That's why we use MediSee.'

'Surely singles would be better?' suggested Wyles.

'Maybe. I suppose, by definition, they're the ones who'd have trouble forming relationships.'

'You know,' put in Samuel, removing a slice of fat from his steak, 'I reckon the ideal candidates would be opposites.'

'How do you mean?' asked Wyles.

'The opposites attract thing?' said Hoskins.

'Yes, one partner that shags everything in sight and one that's, well, too picky. So neither of them could form decent relationships – but for completely opposite reasons.'

'Better still,' added Samuel, 'two people who hate the bloody sight of each other.'

'Get me and the missus down there, then!' joked Delaney. 'We'd be perfect.'

The waitress came round, they all ordered more drinks and such idle, if pleasant, speculation petered out as they got back onto the altogether more serious subject of golf handicaps.

This continued for a good twenty minutes, but as the yarns and anecdotes diminished, first Amraj, then Theo Hoskins and finally William Wyles took leave for a pee.

In the gents, their paths overlapped and, whilst looking reverently downward – one zipping up, one winkling out, one shaking off – they sighed and spoke of the necessity to return to work. But Wyles' mind was obviously still on earlier matters: 'Tell you what,' he said to Amraj, 'We're giving them a visit, aren't we?'

'Who's that?'

'MediSee. You know, during the trials.'

'Oh yes, on er… ' He couldn't recall the exact date, so he just shrugged. 'Some time during the second week, I forget the exact day – I'll ask Michelle when we get back.'

'Thanks, but, er, I was thinking,' Wyles paused by the mirror, probing a filling with a toothpick.

'Thinking what?' asked Amraj.

'Well, we could ask them how things were going.'

'Well, yes, we will.'

'No, not just the trials. You know, how things were… you know, how they were getting on together – the trialists, I mean.'

'Oh, I see, you mean their relationships?'

'Yes, anything… couples that look, you know, interesting.'

Amraj curled his lip negatively at this. 'Not so sure about that Will. They'll be looking at other things. And it's a double-blind, remember.'

'But it'll be un-blinded when the trials are all over, won't it?'

'True.'

'So we could ask them to put a line or two about relationships in the report. I don't mean anything specific. Just generally…'

'Maybe,' he shrugged. 'But they are supposed to be looking at anti-depressants.'

'I know that. But surely somewhere in the summary, or maybe at the start, they could say something about the general mood, at least.'

'Maybe,' replied Amraj, yet again curling his lip in doubt. As a scientific man, he couldn't see it. For him, such concepts as 'general mood' just didn't cut it. But he'd do as he was told though. He always did.

Lily

Y ou may recall that it was on a Friday, after I'd picked up that copy of *The Big Issue*, that this story really started. But it was on a far later Friday, after a first full week at MediSee, that the story *really* began to happen. In a way I never, ever could have predicted.

Up until then it had all been pretty uneventful. And in many ways this day was no different, although I'd had a really good night's sleep and had woken up feeling far more refreshed than usual. It's difficult to explain, but, I suppose, I felt more at peace with the world. Maybe it was the medication, maybe it wasn't. Either way, everything and everyone seemed to be that little bit more tranquil.

I ate my usual breakfast of muesli and fruit, talking with Francine about nothing in particular. She then went off to do something or other and I took my coffee to my customary place on the sofa. On the way there I said good morning to Tim, who was plugged into his iPod, then to Josh, who was quietly strumming his guitar, then Chris, who was cradling a Kindle, and finally to Vicky and Jasmine, who were thumbing through magazines.

I settled down, opened my book and started reading. It was a book called *The Road* by Cormac McCarthy and I couldn't really get into it. It seemed to be a little heavy for the mood I was in – though it had seemed perfect a couple of days earlier. So I closed it again and put it on my knee.

It was then that Ben came in. I'm pretty sure he didn't stop at the breakfast table and, from recollection, he didn't say much to any of the others either – just a few good mornings and hello's. And the last thing I expected was for him to come straight over to me. But that's exactly what he did.

You see, the area where I tended to sit was like a little enclave, well away from the TV and the video games. It consisted of a sofa, a few chairs and a coffee table. As I mentioned earlier, it's amazing how soon we claim our little spaces and make our little camps. Perhaps it goes way back to nest building or something. Whatever the reason, what I can say is that during the course of the day certain people would make this area theirs. This would mainly consist of me, Francine and Sophie, plus maybe Johnny and Russ. The opposite camp – noisier, TV watching, game playing – consisted of Chris, Brendan, Dom and Ben – plus any of their friends who turned up. Then there was a sort of crossover group, who would put appearances in both camps. They were Vicky, Jasmine, Claudia and Tim. Finally, there was Josh, the guitar-playing loner, who fitted into no category and was seemingly happiest with his own company.

So the last person I really expected to kick the day off with – a day which had started so peacefully – was someone from the head banger's guild; someone who, come to think of it, was pretty much head banger-in-chief.

As he drew close, I found myself re-opening my book and looking down at it. I didn't really want the contact. At least, I didn't think I did.

'Sorry,' is what he said.

I simply looked up at him.

'For last night, I mean.'

'That's, erm, alright,' I said, and looked back down again.

I kind of expected that to be that. I mean, it really wasn't that big a deal in the first place. In fact, in a funny way, his apology made me feel worse. I must have given a more vicious rant than I'd thought. But then he surprised me even more: 'No, it was stupid. I hope you got back to sleep.'

'Yes, it was no problem. I was awake anyway.'

'Well, anyway, like I said. I'm sorry.'

He then turned and left. I watched him walk away. Somehow, he seemed, well, different, but I can't quite say how. Then he stopped, turned and said: 'Good book, by the way.'

'You've read it?'

'Yes, it's got a great ending.' He then smiled and said: 'But don't worry, I won't tell you.'

'Actually, I've hardly started,' I replied. 'I'm kind of struggling with it.'

He retraced the few steps he'd made and pulled up one of the chairs opposite.

'Yes, it is a bit weird at first, but it's worth sticking with it.'

This fascinated me. I wouldn't, for one minute, have had Ben down as much of a reader. And certainly not of a book that had been described by *The Guardian* as 'a modern masterpiece'.

'Have you read many of his books?' I asked.

'No,' he replied. 'I hadn't even heard of him. I don't read many books. Saw the movie on DVD and didn't really rate it. But someone recommended the actual book, so...'

He then settled back and added: 'When I do read I like American stuff, so it fits the bill there too.'

Now that impressed me. Rather than spouting on about how well read he was – the kind of thing I might even have done – he pretty much admitted the opposite. Mind you, up until then I'd have been impressed to find he'd read a bloody Superman comic.

'So who do you like? American-wise, I mean?'

'Well, maybe Bukowsky; have you heard of him?'

I certainly had. I'd read a book of his called *Women* and hated it. He was a total misogynist. Alcoholic too. I suppose I should have told him that; said how crap his choice of author was, but out of politeness, I just said: 'I, um, did read one of his books and found it... how can I put it...?'

'You don't sound too impressed.'

'Well he wasn't exactly a charmer, was he?'

'True,' conceded Ben.

I asked him why he liked him so much and he said that when he'd read *Ham on Rye* he found himself 'sort of identifying with him' which was rather worrying. Worse still, he followed that up with: 'I think it would be easy for me to be like that.' Some answer! Apart from anything else, Bukovsky was a total loser. I suppose Ben's answer told me one of two things. Either he was admitting to having genuine problems in his life. Or he was trying to impress me by claiming to be some kind hell-raiser. Ten minutes earlier I would have put money on it being the latter. But now I wasn't so sure. Mind you, neither option seemed particularly attractive. Yet he, strangely, suddenly did.

'What do you mean by it would be easy for you to be like him?'

'Well,' he shrugged, 'to just give in, I suppose.'

'Give in?' I asked.

He then thought for a bit and said: 'It's difficult to explain, but if you have to ask the question, you probably don't have the problem.'

This was all getting a bit obscure, particularly for a first meeting. It could have been rather pretentious too. But for some reason it simply wasn't. He was being very frank, completely genuine.

'Actually,' he added, 'thinking about it, most stories are like that, aren't they? I mean, it's kind of "there but for the grace of God". Even thrillers are based on people in problem situations, aren't they?' He then paused, thought again, and added: 'I think there's a word for it, but I can't remember what it is.'

'Schadenfreude?' I suggested.

'Probably,' he answered, adding: 'I'm crap with poncey words like that.'

I was fractionally offended, and my body language possibly showed it. I really hadn't intended to sound poncey, as he put it. And after all, he did ask! On the other hand, he probably wouldn't have said it so openly if he thought I was trying to be clever.

Then it became apparent that similar thought had gone through his head: 'Oh, I'm, er, sorry. I didn't mean… it's just isn't my sort of word.'

'Well it certainly isn't mine,' I said. 'But you did ask.'

'Yes, you're right, I did… and I'm sorry.' He then smiled and added: 'Again.'

'No,' I said, 'I was probably being touchy. It's, er, in my job description – poncey words, I mean.'

'Oh yes, what's that?'

'English teacher, I'm afraid.'

'Right. Proper job.'

So I asked him what he did, and he told me he was in advertising, with the emphasis on '*was*', and he went on to tell me a rather sorry tale about how he'd been riding the crest of a wave (even *I* knew some of the ads he'd made!) and how it had all come to an abrupt end. 'Thought I was fireproof,' he said, laughing darkly. 'Until I was fired.'

I said all the right things – you know, about being sure he'd get a job before long.

We did have something in common though: English. Okay, so I had to know the technicalities – the grammar and the posh words – but his skill was far greater. In my job I had a whole lesson to get a point over. He had just thirty seconds.

He finally left at about eleven o'clock. I know it was that time because I looked at my watch. I just couldn't believe we'd been talking for over an hour – it seemed like about ten minutes. He still hadn't had anything to eat and the breakfast had been cleared away. So he made for the vending machine and left me to my book.

We reconvened at lunchtime, sitting next to each other for the very first time. Actually, I must confess, I'd timed it that way. Had he too? Must have come as a surprise to Francine and Sophe – I'd moaned about him on more than one occasion.

I had some salad and told him about my family, and he had some curry and he told me about his – such as it was. Apparently, on his dad's side, he had two half-brothers and a half-sister. Not only did these three half-siblings have a different mother to him, but they had a different mother to each other, too. Oh yes and he had no contact with any of them – half-brothers, half-sister or dad. He still saw his mum, though. But not as often as he'd have liked to. Oh yes, and he had half-siblings on her side too, but it was all getting a little bit complicated by then. He told me that one of the few benefits of his newly unemployed status was that he should be able to see a bit more of his mum. Apparently she still lived in the same area that he'd been bought up in – Walworth, in south London – or, as he put it: 'I tell people I was conceived in Walworth and they think I'm talking about a bankrupt store – which, knowing my mum, could well be true.'

All things considered, I reckon he'd done quite well for himself, yet he was pretty self-deprecating – wouldn't even take credit for climbing the advertising ladder.

'Badge of honour being working class on the Creative floor,' he said. 'All jocks, Geordies and Scousers – complete opposite on the Accounts floor.'

Yet again, time had flown. I looked up to find that, with Ben next to me, the entire seating arrangement changed. Russ now sat next to Sophe, Johnny was with Francine and Brendan partnered Vicky. On the other table I noticed that Chris and Jasmine were getting on well. Even lonesome, guitar strumming Josh found himself deep in conversation with vague, distant Claudia. So with the exception of gay Tim, who was happily chatting to a boy called Tommy – who was visiting for the day – it was boy, girl, boy, girl, boy, girl, right round both tables.

My Mum couldn't have arranged it better.

Ben

I slept well, but when I awoke, slowly drowsing on my pillow, there was something way, way at the back of my mind. In those first seconds, before waking thoughts took over, I had a feeling that something was missing. Then, as my brain came round, the idea began to form. I don't know if it came from a dream, because I couldn't remember dreaming, but wherever it came from, I knew I had to speak to that Lily girl. I had to say sorry. Making a noise outside someone's room probably seems like a trivial thing to have on your mind when you wake up, and it wasn't my normal style at all, but I suppose small things can loom large when you're sealed away from the real world and you've got nothing much else to think about.

I lay there, eyes closed, picturing her face – thinking about what I'd say and how I'd say it. Would she think it was odd? After all, it wasn't *that* big a deal. Then a thought came to me. Was that really the reason I wanted to talk to her?

I opened my eyes, eased myself up. Looking down the ward: just mounds of snoring bed linen. For once, I was one of the first up. I dropped my legs out of bed, sat on the bed and yawned – and stretched. Then stood up and stretched again. I got my dressing gown and ambled to the bathroom. I looked at my reflection in the mirror. Me. The only one I'll ever know. I cleaned my teeth thoroughly. Then I splashed water on my face. Me, but wet. Next came shaving foam. Steadily, I shaved. Why are you doing this, Ben?

You know, I chat up girls all the time. Or used to. But that was mostly in clubs and bars, screaming into ears, drunk, showing off. And half the time they were drunk and showing off too – and screaming into my ear, if I was lucky.

Lucky? Why is it called a one night stand? The last thing either of you are capable of doing is standing.

This was different. This time, I liked a girl – Lily – who didn't seem to like me. In fact, she probably hated me. Which was understandable. So did I.

I showered, toweled myself, sprayed on deodorant, patted on after-shave and walked back to the ward. Then I sat on the bed again and thought. You know, primary contact shouldn't be a problem. I could do that. It was *meaningful* contact I'd never done.

Okay Ben, so you're just about to leave your comfort zone. So what? You've done that all your life, in different ways. Yes, but what should I actually say?

Then it struck me. 'Sorry.' That's it! 'Sorry.' One word. I felt invigorated. Or perhaps it was all just the shower.

I zipped up my jeans, pulled on a clean tee shirt, walked back to the shower room and gave the mirror one last check. Passable. Okay Ben, *go*.

As I'd hoped – or perhaps feared – Lily was where she usually was, sitting at the far end of the room. I wandered through, saying a few hello's on the way and, because she had her head in a book, got right up to her without her even noticing.

I coughed but she still didn't look up, so I just went for it: 'Sorry.' She half-closed her book and looked up at me. I don't recall her saying much, just looked at me with those eyes. So I said it again. She replied with something like 'Okay', or 'no problem', or something, but whatever it was, it was pretty dismissive. And that was it. Then she put her head back into her book.

I was still pleased I'd done it, even if she never spoke to me again. There was something about her. It was almost as if I knew her, but I couldn't quite put a finger on it.

Anyway, I noticed what she was reading and it was then that I told her a lie. Pretty impressive, eh? The first word I say to her is sorry and the second is a lie.

But I was so used to it that it just came out naturally. Reflex action.

You see, it's a game you play. In media, anyway. You don't actually read award-winning novels, or see art house movies, or buy obscure albums but you do flip through reviews, watch trailers and hang out in the right places – and pretend you have. Sad isn't it. But like I said, it happened in a flash; just as I was turning away and just as she was looking back down at the book. 'Good book,' I said.

I think she was impressed. Well, that's the whole point, isn't it? Then I brought up another book; a book I *had* read. And that's another smartarse trick. Quickly move the conversation onto something you *do* know about, something you *have* read. Shitty and shabby, but effective. After all, I got to talk to her and that was the main point. So misconception accomplished.

I do hope I didn't come over as a smartarse though, but I don't think I did. As I said, there was something about her that fascinated me, so I was genuinely interested in what she thought – what her opinions were.

Actually, at one point, I thought I'd completely blown it. On two counts! Firstly, we were talking about books and she didn't seam too impressed with my choice of author. Then I completely put my foot in it over something she said. She said something like schaden freuline – which was a word I'd heard of and I kind of knew what it meant, but I'd never use a word like that because it's way too poncey. And rather stupidly, that's exactly what I said. I suppose you'd call it faux pas – except that's poncey too. Either way, that's what I said. So just to recap; in my first meeting with her I needed to apologise for waking her up, then I lied, then I brought up an author she hated and finally I insulted her. Great start, Ben.

So it was a bit of a result finding myself sitting next to her at lunch. Result, but not luck. I was watching out for her. I asked if I could join her. I mean, there was a gap. And she said yes. So I got in there!

I managed to get through the whole meal without insulting her or telling her a load of old bollocks. Actually, that's not entirely true because most of what I say is a load of old bollocks anyway. But at least in this case it was a load of old true bollocks. I told her some stuff about my family, and she told me some stuff about her and her family. They sounded entirely different to my lot. Normal. They spoke to each other and knew who their partner's were and stuff.

She comes from Beckenham, in Kent. Geographically, that's not very far from where I was brought up. Geographically. Her mum and dad are still together. I need to repeat that line because it's an alien concept. You see, these two people got married and bought a nice house in the suburbs. Then they had two daughters. The youngest was Lily and she's thirty-ish. Therefore the oldest would be, say, thirty-five. So these two people have been married for thirty-five years *at least* and they're *still together*. Amazing!

Later that afternoon we paired up again, this time for a game of Scrabble against Francine and Johnny. One plus was that it put the whole poncey word thing to bed – you know, the whole schaden-whatsit thing – because Lily jokingly suggested that we should have special bonus points for poncey words. You know, if someone could come up with a *zeitgeist* or a *recherché* or some such, they'd get a double word score for sheer poncey-ness. This got a bit of a laugh and, like I said, put the whole issue to bed. None of us did, as it happens – though I did come up with *duvet*.

As the day wore on it wasn't just us four that were getting on well together. Russ, Sophe, Brendan and Vicky were playing Trivial Pursuit on the dining table, Chris and Jasmine were playing video games on the telly and Josh was teaching guitar to Claudia. Somehow the whole place seemed to be sort of calming down, leveling off. Or perhaps it was just me. Or Lily. Either way, something was bloody happening.

I've never really rated the expression 'getting on like a house on fire'. Exploding houses are way too violent. So I'll just say we got on like a house. A house where you just *had* to get on.

A house you couldn't ask anyone out on dates from, because there was no 'out', no 'dates' and no 'from.' A place with no post-date texting games – all that 'who should text first' and 'how long to reply' stuff – because there was no point in texting someone in the same room. And no point in emailing either. Or Facebooking. No booze, no drugs, no parties. The only ammunition I had was talk. I needed to take it slowly though. Which could mean she didn't think I was that interested – or perhaps gay or just plain shy.

But I suppose, all things considered, I'd take shyness. If that was the only fault she could find in me, I'll take it.

Ben Dryden shy? What was going on!

Dr Francis Taylor

D r Francis Taylor's working days were as regular as his bowel movements. And, as a man of both medicine and science, he considered the two to be inextricably linked.

Probably the most regular of all his workaday routines, apart from the colonic ones, were his lunch breaks. Exactly one hour in duration and equidistant from the day's start to the day's end, it provided him with both sustenance and, should he want it (and mostly he did), a little solitude. At least, normally it did. Normally, he could eat his sandwiches, browse philatelic magazines and take a short stroll along the Southbank, where he could, rather appropriately, hum one of his favourite songs – *Waterloo Sunset* – and remember his youth.

But that Monday was different. On that Monday, a group of suits from CalmerCeutical were visiting, so just for once his routine would have to be broken.

As ever on these tiresome occasions, he did and said all the right things. He greeted them with handshakes, introduced Nurse Harty, overviewed the progress, toured wards, met inmates and expertly guided them back to his office, to where they all sat down to a light, working luncheon of Pret A Manger and Evian. None of this was a problem – though he certainly favoured his normal pilchard over the crayfishy things that Angela had arranged. But what he couldn't abide were the ridiculously trite pleasantries. He wasn't interested in William Wyles' golf handicap, and quite clearly William Wyles felt the same way about his stamps. So why the pretence? And then there were the others.

Why must he discuss his family holiday in Devon with someone whose title was Corporate Strategist (MBA) and whose name he couldn't even remember? What had that got to do with medicine? How did that push the boundaries of science?

Oh well, he thought, as Angela handed round the coffee. It'll all soon be over and then perhaps I'll be allowed one remaining lunchtime pleasure: a Muller Light (prune) – hopefully still stashed in the fridge – and a glance at *Gibbons Monthly*.

But it wasn't all bad. At least Dr Amraj Singe, the one member of the group who was scientifically grounded, seemed to want to keep the conversation on matters medical. And once that idiot of a CEO had finished going on about his bloody six iron, it was Dr Singe who mercifully asked how things were shaping up on the wards.

He was pleased to report that things were indeed shaping up well, though he also reminded them that they were barely halfway through the trials and that they hadn't really started collating the data. They all understood this, of course, but Dr Singe pushed him, asking him if he had any other observations.

'Other observations?' replied Dr Taylor, briefly lost in thought about his yoghurt.

'Well, you know, on the patients.'

Dr Taylor bit his lip thoughtfully, but couldn't really think of anything in particular. Then he said: 'Well, one of them, Ben Dryden, came in a little worse for wear. He'd been out drinking the night before. I thought I might have a few problems with him, but he's knuckled down well. But no, apart from that, nothing comes to mind.'

'Okay, but I was thinking more of, well,' Amraj paused for thought, before adding: 'How they've been interacting – you know, together.'

'Interacting?' questioned Dr Taylor.

'What he means, Francis,' interjected Wyles, smoothly, 'is how they're getting on with *each other*. You know, relationship-wise.'

Dr Taylor, rubbed his chin, thought, then observed: 'Pretty well, I suppose. Everyone's pretty jolly. We keep a tight ship, you know. Don't stand for any nonsense.'

William Wyles thought for a second. This clearly wasn't going anywhere. As a boss, sometimes you just have to go in with all guns blazing. 'Well, yes, Francis I realize that, but what Amraj is asking is – put it this way: Have you noticed any romantic relationships developing?'

'Romantic relationships?'

If anything, this seemed to confuse Dr Taylor even more. Words like 'romantic' and 'relationship' were completely outside his remit.

'Erm, Mr Wyles?' asked the doctor.

'Call me Will,' said Wyles, leaning back in his chair.

'Oh yes, Will. I'm, er, still not sure I'm exactly following you. Why would we be concerned with... ' He stopped short, hardly wanting to utter the words, 'with *Romantic Relationships?*'

At that point, Amraj came back into the conversation. This pussyfooting about was getting them nowhere. So he decided to start again from the very beginning. He told Dr Taylor about the early research and the first tests they did. Then he mentioned the oxytocin and the dopamine and the pheromone. He even touched on the androstadienones.

This was probably the tack they should have taken in the first place. After all, Francis Taylor wasn't the type of man who was comfortable with all that all that touchy-feely stuff. But he was quite prepared to buy into the science of it and, as Amraj pointed out, if emotions have physiological effects on our bodies – increased heartbeat, hot flushes, breathlessness – why not the reverse; physics having emotional effects? And whilst romantic relationships weren't really Dr Taylors's cup of tea, androstadienones certainly were.

And so after listening patiently for perhaps a full, silent five minutes, his only response to Amraj, right at the end of his monologue, was a slow, fascinated: 'I see.' This was followed by a thoughtful and considered: 'Interesting. Yes, I *do* see.'

That afternoon, after the little delegation had left, the hours simply flew by. He decided that some aspects of this new assignment were probably better left to Nurse Angela.

Women were far better at that sort of thing. She could wander the wards with a sort of liaison list. Yes, that sounded the part. He could then process the data and perhaps tag along from time to time – though only in an observational capacity, obviously.

So he'd do all his normal stuff: administer drugs, check blood pressure, tick charts, whilst she could do the bedside chit-chat – look for the telltale signs. Perhaps he could even come up with something for checking romantic neural activity too, if it existed. He could look that one up.

That afternoon, he and Harty did the first of these little forays and he was amazed what his nurse picked up on. Whereas he saw a normal girl, Angela saw freshly plucked eyebrows and newly administered lipstick. And as for the boys, he noted absolutely nothing at all, whilst she noted combed hair and a proliferation of that most unlikely male accessory, clean underpants. Furthermore, according to her, at least six of them – boys and girls – had 'that look in their eyes' – whatever that meant.

'You know, Francis,' she said, sipping her tea, 'I do think they could be onto something here.'

'Yes?'

'Yes. I mean, even you'll admit that the atmosphere over the last few days has been, well, tranquil, to say the least.'

'Yes Angela,' he conceded, looking at her over his glasses. 'But we are effectively testing tranquilizers.'

'True, but some of the patients, well…'

He took off his glasses and said: 'Go on.'

'Well, Russell and Sophie, for a start. And Claudia has certainly taken to Josh's guitar lessons.'

'Umm, but it's all a bit subjective isn't it. Nothing to get your teeth into.'

'Nature of the beast, Francis. Love isn't easily captured. It's like…'

Angela thought for a while, but was unable to come up with what love was actually like. Then suddenly said: 'I know: Like a butterfly. Love is like a butterfly.'

'Oh yes, I remember that one.'

'Wendy Craig,' she smiled, before softly trilling: '*Love is like a butterfly, soft and gentle as a sigh…*'

Saints preserve us, he thought, the place had gone stark raving mad. There again, it was all quite interesting – scientifically, that is.

'So what about Tim, for instance? I certainly haven't seen him, well… you know… swooning around with anyone.'

'There was that visitor. Keith, I think.'

'Keith! You mean… ?'

Nurse Angela sighed wearily. Male doctors, she thought, must be the world's most unobservant beings. Which, if you think about it, is a little worrying.

'Anyway, Francis, it's not just about swooning. Love plays havoc with hormones. There's downs as well as ups.'

'Doesn't with mine.'

'With respect, Francis, you and Mary have been married quite a long time now and…'

'Thirty-seven years.'

'Exactly.'

Dr Taylor thought for a second. Not about Mary - he never thought about her during working hours. No, he was thinking about the patients.

'So Angela, who would you say are showing signs of an emotional downside, then?'

She considered this before answering: 'Well, that Lily girl, for example. I'm pretty sure that she's been seeing a lot of that Ben recently, and yet she was very quiet tonight.'

Dr Taylor thought about this. She certainly wasn't herself; not her normal bright self at all. 'So you're saying that if a patient is all starry-eyed he or she could be in love, and if he or she is down in the dumps, he or she could *also* be love. Not exactly scientific, is it?'

'No Francis, it's not; as I said before… ' She wafted her hands a little and quietly repeated her earlier serenade: '*Love is like a butterfly, soft and gentle as a sigh…*'

For God's sake, not again. Then, as she repeated this same verse for a third time, his face lightened up. He suddenly remembered. Life wasn't so bad after all. His prune yoghurt was still in the fridge.

Lily

Had I been a fourteen-year-old, and had I kept a diary the way fourteen-year-olds do, the entries during the first half of that second week would have gone something like: 'Monday Ben!', 'Tuesday Ben, Ben!!!', 'Wednesday Ben, Ben, Ben!!!!!'. And as well twenty Bens and fifty exclamation marks, there would probably have been sugar pink hearts and kisses written in one of those sparkly silver markers. But I'm not fourteen, and nothing is sugar pink or sparkly – or even black and white.

In the evenings, in my bed, I found myself weighing up and wondering. Was Ben? Was I? Were we? We spent loads of time together: talking and laughing and sometimes, well, neither. And after all, happiness in silence is always a good sign. But I still wasn't sure. The good news was that I liked him, and I was pretty sure he liked me. But in MediSee, the means of showing it, and taking things to another level, somehow weren't available. At least, that was my reasoning.

Okay, sex-wise, there could have been loads of opportunities. We were in a building full of beds, *and* I had a private room. But we certainly hadn't *had* sex and, anyway, that's not exactly what I meant. I meant, we hadn't... well, even kissed. How Edwardian is that?

And if that last statement 'hadn't even kissed' sounds like a fourteen-year-old's diary again, so be it. That's the way it was.

You see, we had no stepping-stones. No walks in the park or drinks in the pub. Of course, the one thing Ben *could* have done was suggest doing all those things when we were out, but he hadn't. Maybe I'm too old-fashioned or something, but if he wasn't asking me, I wasn't asking him.

It occurred to me that phones, or lack of them, had a part to play in all this. I would imagine that for a bloke it's far easier setting up a first date, or perhaps a second date, by phone or text. Okay, we all had them and were allowed to use them, but it would have been ridiculous because we saw each other all the time.

Was he worrying about the same things? Probably not. Most likely, if men fancy a shag, they just go for it, come what may. So to speak.

You know, my first impression of him was that he was a wham-bam merchant. Not that I wanted a wham-bam merchant. But I didn't have him down as the perfect gentleman either; which was exactly the way he was behaving. Too perfect, in fact. Which may, of course, have meant he wasn't interested. Unless he was gay, which I was pretty sure he wasn't.

Had we been in the real world, would I have slept with him by now? Probably. Does that surprise you? After all, I'd only known him a few days and I'm certainly no bed-hopper. But during those few days we'd spent a good fifty hours together – and I do mean good. We'd spoken of families and friends and hopes and fears. And when you look at it that way, how many dates would it take to build up that kind of relationship?

The whole clinical trial environment, if you'd wished it to be, was like some kind of relationship hothouse – but without the hot bits. I can imagine what you're thinking: relationship without the hot bits, what else *is* there? Good question – and I haven't got an answer. But whatever else it was, it was there, in MediSee, in spades. The whole atmosphere was weird, yet sort of wonderful. Unless it was the medication or something.

Which brings me to the other question. Would I have been any happier if I *had* slept with him? Or would I have simply have been worrying about that instead? Oh, the angst of it all!

As I lay there, not focusing on my book, I just wanted to be fourteen again. Why couldn't it all be sugar pink hearts and exclamation marks?

I put my bookmark in the page and closed it.

So there were positives and there were negatives. And that's where I stood, or perhaps didn't stand.

I turned the lights out and snuggled down.

The whole 'taking it on to another stage' thing would just have to wait until we were in the outside world again. But would he still be interested? I had no way of guessing and, apart from giving him the big old come on – enticing him into my room wearing nothing but a skimpy negligee, I couldn't see how that was ever going find that out. And anyway, what would that have told me?

I wriggled my arms and legs into a different position. It's funny how, in bed, the perfect body position and the coolest of sheets soon become less than cool, so you have to move on again. A metaphor, maybe?

In the dark, under the sheets, I carried on thinking. All that skimpy negligee stuff just wasn't me. And anyway, I hadn't even packed one – didn't even *own* one. My sexiest nighttime wear was what I had on – Wind In The Willows jimjams. And they were Winceyette!

I wriggled my body again and half threw off the sheets. The whole scenario was just too confusing and contradictory. On the one hand I might have found the one thing I'd been looking for – the thing all that Internet dating had failed to find. And on the other I might have found absolutely nothing.

Lying there, I did make up my mind about one thing though. The next morning I'd do the one thing I should have done earlier. Talk it all over with other girls.

Ben

By the middle of my second week things were definitely looking up. I'd managed to stick to my no booze rule, my sleep was improving and my mood was way better. I'd also made a few friends – Johnny and Francine, Russ and Sophe – but most of all there was Lily. For me, she was the best thing to come along for a long, long time. Better than a goal at Millwall (at the right end, that is, which is pretty rare) better than a line and even better than a gold at Cannes. I remember Ned once saying: 'If you can't stick it *in* the net, *up* your nose, or *on* the mantelpiece, it ain't worth having.' And that was me, just a few weeks earlier. Not now. And most of that change, perhaps *all* of that change, was down to Lily.

There was one slight downer though. There always is, isn't there? I still hadn't plucked up enough courage to, well, to do anything about it. Apart from just talk, that is. Which was most unlike me – or most unlike the old me.

The thing was I didn't want to make a twat of myself. Ridiculous, isn't it? A bloke who spends his time coming up with daft ideas and falling off of bar stools, didn't want to make a fool of himself. But it wasn't only that. It was also the rejection thing. What if I'd asked her out and she said thanks, but no thanks? What if the last few days hadn't been that special for her at all – and I was just a bloke who'd helped to while away a boring week? What if I tell her how I feel and she just laughs? That would probably be the hardest thing of all. Crushing.

But I was pretty sure she did like me. You see, we were so on the same wavelength. Okay, we were from very different backgrounds, but that didn't seem to matter.

For instance: travelling. She'd been to all the places I hadn't and vice versa. Also, I'd done them on the grand scale – the business class and the chauffeured pick up – whereas she'd done bucket shops and hostels. Yet her experiences, and certainly the way she described them, seemed more interesting.

But, in a way, that's not the point I'm making. The main point is that we *were* talking about that sort of stuff, but we weren't sparring. Not competing; completing. And that's not the way it had always been – with me, anyway. I have a tendency, or *had* a tendency, to have no interest in what the other person was saying – only in what *I* was saying. Anything you can say, I can say better.

I can't speak for girls on this one, of course, but that's certainly the way it can be with blokes – even when you're chatting up birds. It's all, impress, impress, impress. If the girl tells a joke, you top it. At least, *you* think you do. But with Lily and me it just wasn't like that. Nothing like that at all.

So that was the good news. But the bad news was that's all it was. All talk, no action. Something was holding me back. And by Wednesday morning, I thought I'd completely blown it. Up till then, it had all been pretty fine, but then I started having doubts. Not doubts about me, doubts about what she really thought of me. At least, Wednesday was when I first noticed them.

It all started when I said good morning to her. That was all I said: 'Morning Lily, you look well,' – or something like that. She just kind of blanked me. Not nastily or anything, that wasn't Lily. She just kind of didn't respond much. And that was the last I saw of her that morning. Up until then we'd been joined at the hip.

The trouble with that sort of thing, is that you don't know if you're the reason why. Now normally I wouldn't care, but with Lily, I did. And the other problem is that you begin to wonder if you've simply been misreading the situation all along. Had I been bigging it all up? Had I been imagining it? Or, perhaps she *was* originally interested, but because I'd played it too cool, for too long, now she *wasn't*. And those two possibilities opened up two more questions. Should I just go for it? Before it's too late, I mean. Or, if I'd been misreading her, would that scare her away even more? Stick or twist?

God, it didn't used to be this complicated. Why is life so fucking difficult?

Lily

MRSA! I ask bloody you! What a stupid reason for not visiting me. Only my sister could come up with that! I mean, I do love Thomas; that's her son, my nephew – well, obviously – but wrapped up in cotton wool, or what! She was concerned the poor little love might catch it. How ridiculous! It was obviously just an excuse. She had no intention of visiting. But why wait till halfway through the second week? And more to the point, why ring at ten o'clock at bloody night! And what really, *really* pissed me off was that I had expressly told her, *expressly* told her, *not* to tell Mum and Dad I was doing medical trials. So what does she do? Yup, you guessed it. Obviously she'd blurted it out, then realized she'd made a mistake. But does she admit that? Of course not. She tries to tell me 'it's best that they should know'. I was seething! Big bloody sisters. No matter what age you are, it's always there – big sister, little sister.

So I tossed and turned all night enraged about her. Then I started thinking about the whole Ben thing. Then it was back to her again. I tell you this, if this stuff can calm you down after a conversation with my sister – give you a good night's sleep after she'd rung up – it certainly *is* a wonder drug.

So that, together with the whole Ben thing, had put paid to my Tuesday night's sleep. And put me in a foul mood on the Wednesday. Oh yes, and I was pre-bloody-menstrual.

So I can't say I woke up because I hadn't been asleep in the first place. I just sort of lay there, floundering in drowsy, sleep deprived semi-consciousness.

Eventually I hauled myself out of bed, showered and cleaned my teeth. I then put on some clothes and tried to concentrate on the image in front of me; the image in the mirror.

What a bloody mess. One night without sleep and my face had turned into putty, my hair into a bird's nest and a pimple had appeared on my chin. I never get pimples!

I did some minor repair work but it wasn't a full service – which didn't really work. Eventually, I gave up and slopped to the breakfast room. If Ben wanted me in my entirety, this was what he'd have to see. '*You're my everything*', goes the song. Well, Ben, I hope you're ready for this, because this is what *my everything* looks like.

He wasn't there, thank God. Only three people at the table. There was Brendan and Vicky, but they were at the far end, and Tim, who, being gay, was just about allowed to see me in this condition. I grunted a reply, spooned some muesli into a bowl, poured some coffee and slumped into a chair.

And that was another thing that was different in here. Out there, in the real world, new boyfriends weren't confronted with images like this first thing in the morning – unless it was a beer shag and therefore deprived of senses. It would take weeks of subjugation before I'd allow a sober male to see me looking crap on a regular basis. And men just don't understand that sort of thing. They think you need a reason to feel crap – an argument, an illness, a bad day at the office. But you don't. Sometimes you just wake up crap.

So what does he say when he bumps into me? 'Morning, Lily.' He comes up behind me, I'm not even prepared – not that that would've made much difference – and says 'Morning, Lily!' Now I know that doesn't *sound* unreasonable, but it was the way he said it! All bright and cheery. 'You look great, Lily' was what he was implying.

Just standing there, sweating from the exercise bike and looking annoyingly hunky. Men really are stupid. Implied or otherwise, I was *not* looking great. I was looking many, many things, but not great. And you know what? If I *had* been looking great, if I'd tried my hardest and was fully scrubbed up, he probably wouldn't have noticed a thing. Men. Are. Stupid.

So I just grunted '*Morning*,' through a mouthful of muesli.

He didn't stay long. I must admit I probably didn't make him that welcome – hardly even looked up from my bowl. Well, I mean, I'm not vain or anything, no shallow bimbo – I do realize there's more to life than looks. But I did have a pimple, and pudgy skin *and* bags under my eyes. I repeat: I was *not looking great.*

Once we'd had our morning medication, I decided there was nothing for it but to go back to bed. I slept for a couple of hours and woke up feeling a little better. Was it the sleep or was it the medication? Or was it simply that my brain had just given up going over the same old questions?

What I *did* decide was to be more positive again. And that idea I'd had the night before, of discussing it with the girls, seemed a really constructive way forward.

When I got back into the dayroom, the boys were playing that Grand Theft Thingamy, and Sophe and Francine were nattering at the table. I suppose the fact that I called Ben, Russ and Johnny 'the boys' tells you quite a lot, because if they were becoming 'the boys', then we three, in my eyes, were 'the girls'. The six of us were turning into a group of couples. Jesus – *group of couples* – some piece of English!

I kind of knew, or guessed, that Sophe and Francine's feelings toward Russ and Johnny were similar to my feelings toward Ben. I didn't need any female intuition because, apart from their body language, Sophe had been spending loads of time with Russ and Francine had already hinted at fancying Johnny. But simply 'fancying' wasn't exactly what I'd been going through. So what did surprise me, particularly as they seemed so much more worldly wise than me, was that they seemed to be facing similar situations. Not only on the loved-up front but on the next stage front too.

Once I'd worked my way into their conversation – a conversation, incidentally, that was already oriented towards Russ and Johnny – it all became much clearer.

'Yeah, I do really like him,' said Francine, nursing a bottle of mineral water. 'But I'm not going to take it any further – not in here, anyway.'

'Uh huh,' I said, running my finger round the rim of my glass.

'You see, it's like I was telling Sophe – maybe it's this place or something – I *do* like him, but…'

She then went onto say pretty much all the things that had been going through my mind – didn't want to get physical yet but wasn't sure why. And just like me, she'd wondered if it was the ward environment. Also just like me, she mentioned the lack of other things: the proper dates and stuff. She even wondered, and this was spookily similar to one of my thoughts, if it was something to do with the drugs we'd been taking.

'And the other thing is the phone,' I added, making the point about our reliance on mobiles.

'Yeah,' agreed Sophe. 'Talking face-to-face sort of moves things forward *and* holds things back at the same time – it's weird.' Which was smack on with my feelings.

It occurred to me that this whole scenario was almost eighteenth century. It had turned us girls into Jane Austin's Bennett sisters and the boys into a bunch of raving Darcys. There again, I'm not sure the Bennett sisters discussed sex quite as openly as we did. I'm not sure eighteenth century gentleman did either – or, come to that, modern day blokes. Properly, I mean.

I can obviously only speak from a female perspective on this but once we girls get going on the physical stuff, we go for it. I reckon we're far more frank. With men, from what I gather, it's all that nudge-nudge, '*I wouldn't mind givin' her one*', stuff. They don't seem to actually discuss sex at all. But anyway, back to us girls. I suppose you might think it a little odd – being close enough, after just a week-and-a-half, to discuss our sex lives. But that was just like the Ben thing. We may all have only known each other for a few days, but we'd probably spent about a year's worth of company together. That, or there was just something in the air.

I must confess at this point that, rather childishly, I found myself feeling a little jealous. You see, ridiculous though it may seem, I envied Sophe because she had indeed gone one step further than I had with Ben. She and Russ had kissed. Ridiculous isn't it? I was actually jealous because one of my friends had snogged a boy and I hadn't. Talk about fourteen-year-olds. Bloody playground stuff! Next, it would be who'd been touched up 'on top' or 'down below'. Actually, on further consideration, that's probably nothing like the playground nowadays. They probably skip the Love Hearts and satchel carrying and go straight for the fifty shades.

Oh yes, and just to underline how adolescent I'd become, I also found myself envious of Francine. This was slightly more reasonable though – but only slightly. You see, Johnny had lined up a post-clinical date with her, exactly as I'd hoped Ben would with me.

So just to recap. I envied Sophe because she'd kissed a boy and Francine because she had a date.

Even so, it's good to know that you're not the only one with worries. And talking of worries, it was Francine who brought up something that really *did* get me thinking.

One of the reasons she gave for not yet having slept with Johnny was that she knew absolutely nothing about him. At first, I found myself feeling a little smug about that. After all, I knew *everything* about Ben, didn't I? But then, as she explained it, I began to wonder.

Her exact words were: 'How do I know Johnny's not married or something?' She went on to explain that usually, when you go out with someone, you might ring them at work or maybe at home. You might then meet them at either of these places and in the process bump into some of their mates or colleagues. Then you go to a pub where there may be more people you know – or he knows. Either way, it's more difficult hiding things. But in the confines of MediSee, everything was make-believe. The outside world just didn't exist. Big Brother with no audience.

So what *did* I know about Ben, apart from what he'd told me? Absolutely nothing. He could have had a wife and three kids; he could be a conman or even a bunny boiler. The only things I knew about him was that he'd been a serial substance abuser – oh, and that his favourite author was a woman-hating alcoholic.

Of course, little old naïve me had never considered all that at all. It had taken the likes of Francine and Sophe, two girls who had men chasing them by the Porsche load, to point this out.

Ben

As I recall, this story started with a hangover in a tube train. But it many ways it starts now.

It was on Wednesday evening of the second week. Only a few hours earlier, I'd decided I'd completely blown it. With Lily, I mean. She'd been in a strange mood all day, avoiding me and generally being grumpy. By the evening, she still wasn't exactly sparkling but she did seem a little brighter. We hadn't spent any time together, you know, just the two of us, but she did tell a group of us – Johnny, Russ, Sophe, Lily and me – that her sister had really pissed her off the night before, so maybe that's why she'd been so moody.

So I made up my mind that unless she became really off with me, I was going to go for it – you know, get her by herself and... and what? Well, whatever gave a clear signal. Ask her out, maybe? We only had a few days left at MediSee so I thought perhaps we could meet up the following weekend somewhere. If she turned me down flat, then so be it.

Anyway, there was bugger all on telly, so we were all sitting round the table, drinking coffee and swapping work stories. I was next to Lily, but there was noticeably more space between us than there had been on previous days. I really couldn't say *why* that was, but it was the *way* it was. Funnily enough though, on that particular table – the kitchen table – it kind of drew us closer. That might sound strange, but because it had rounded ends and because we were almost a metre apart, we were practically sitting opposite each other – you know, kind of like at a restaurant; eye-to-eye.

92

We'd all been talking about funny work incidents; puking up at Christmas parties, photocopying bums, that sort of stuff – and Lily pitched in with a story about something that had happened at an English school she'd worked at in Bournemouth.

She leaned forward and cradled her coffee: 'In the afternoons we had these Communication Lessons,' she said, with a bit of sparkle back in her eyes, 'and instead of endless grammar and stuff the students were supposed to actually *use* their English – you know, in role-plays and stuff. Fortunately, I had the advanced group.'

It was great to hear her on form again, back to her old self, or the self that I'd come to know, anyway.

'Of course,' she continued, taking a sip from her coffee, 'it's much easier having a discussion with an advanced group – their English is better. Well anyway, I'd set a theme of 'Relationships' – you know, love and marriage and stuff. So I put the students into pairs and I asked them to imagine that they were partners, as in romantic partners. And I started by pointing out that in English we don't really have a word for long-term relationships – if we're not married, that is.'

'What about "girlfriend and boyfriend"?' asked Sophe.

'Yes,' agreed Lily, 'But not if they're, like, 40, with two kids.'

'True,' replied Sophe.

'Yeah,' agreed Francine 'Mum sometimes calls Tone her boyfriend and I think it sounds a bit, you know, soppy.'

'So what about "partner"?' offered Johnny.

'Yeah, but they could be a business partners,' shrugged Lily.

'Suppose so,' he said.

I was happy just to watch her talking – to let her hold centre stage – and let the others do the butting in.

'So anyway,' she continued, with a smile back in her voice, 'because they had good English, I asked them to be creative, come up with their own words for relationships. I always tell students that English is a living language – new words come up all the time – so if you *can* think of a better phrase, use it. You know, even if it's a bit near the mark.'

'What about, say… ' said Russ, thinking for a second, 'bollock-naked – would you teach that in class?'

'Yeah,' added Johnny, 'And shit-faced?'

'And twat features?' countered Russ, each coming up with more and more juvenile phrases.

'Of course, why not?' shrugged Lily. 'After all, if they're going to work in an English environment, they'd need the vocabulary…'

'Certainly do where I work,' observed Russ.

Lily smiled at this. 'And anyway, I'd boarded all this relationship vocabulary to help: you know, serious relationship, lover, companion. I also included words like "platonic" because some relationships are sexual and some aren't.'

'Not my bloody office,' added Russ.

This got a few laughs, but Lily just ploughed on: 'Oh yes, and I gave them some more sort of slangy, casual stuff like "one night stand" and "friends with benefits". Surprise, surprise they already knew all that. Generational thing, I suppose – you know, movies and things. So I then gave them about ten minutes to come up with something – told them to imagine that they were at a party and I was their boss. I put on some quiet music, told them to partner up, and we all mingled. I was expecting introductions like "This is my Life Friend", et cetera, but the first student I got to was a German boy called Helmut. He was okay, but a little mixed up. Anyway, he stood up, clicked his heels, gestured towards his partner and said: "*Hi. I'm Helmut and this is Ingrid, she's my serious night stand.*"'

Cue laughs all round.

A little later, after a couple more of us told work related-stories – not half as good as Lily's, she said: 'I think I'm going to get an early night – had a crap one last night.'

'I'll come with you,' I said, and walked beside her to her room.

We didn't say anything as we walked, but when she pushed open her door I said: 'Um Lily, I wondered if we could meet up – you know, after we're out of this place.'

I think I might have been looking at the floor at the time; I certainly didn't have eye contact.

'I'd love to,' she replied.

I looked up, straight at her. Eye-to-eye. I know it sounds corny, particularly as we'd already spent so much time together, but my heart actually skipped a beat.

There was a brief pause, a moment in time, when nothing happened. Then we kissed. I couldn't say who instigated, both of us, possibly. Then we kissed again, and then again – falling into her room… and onto her bed.

We slept for a few hours, entangled. When morning came, grey, through the tiny, high-up window, I got up and dressed. She lay there silently. Sleeping. At least, I thought she was. But when I looked up from pulling a sock on, she was watching me, smiling. She hadn't moved – still had her head on the pillow.

Then she quietly whispered: 'Would you like to be my serious night stand?'

I walked back over, sat on the bed, leaned over and kissed her.

'I was hoping, perhaps, I already was,' is all I replied.

Proof of Liaison

'Two fifty a day, plus expenses,' confirmed Pamela Andrews. 'And with the subjects spread over London, it'll take a while.'

'So, er, how much do you…?'

'Let me see, er…'

Andrews started counting the names: 'There's one, two, three… '

'Fourteen,' interrupted Wyles, saving her the trouble. 'Seven couples.'

'So that should take… oh, about a month, maybe more,' said Andrews.

She waited for the flinch, but it didn't come.

'So I make that about five grand,' he said.

'Possibly,' said Andrews, 'Plus expenses.'

'So if we could confirm five and a half?'

She thought about this. Unlike some of her other cases, this didn't sound particularly high profile, or one of those heartstrings pro bonos. On the other hand, it could be a bit of an earner. So at least if met the last of the big three: goodwill, good press or good money. The fourth, by the way, being goodbye.

'It's, er, hard to be precise,' she said, 'given the numbers… of people, I mean.'

Typical woman, thought Wyles: costly *and* vague. He hated wooliness – could get that back home, for free.

'Look, Mrs Andrews…'

'Ms,' she corrected. 'But you can call me Pamela.'

'Okay, Pamela. I can live with perhaps six, *just*. But I can't have this just dragging on.'

Now if you've guessed that Pamela Andrews is a private eye and that William Wyles is her client, you'd be absolutely right. But if you're picturing her as some Yellow Pages divorce jock, you'd be wrong.

The Andrews Agency had a track record second to none. Finding people was their game – succeeding, on occasions, where the police couldn't. But apart from missing persons, she also dealt with messy relationships. So given Wyles' requirements, a perfect match.

'Okay,' she said, after thinking about it. 'Fixed fee. I might get Anna involved, it'll speed things up a little.'

Better and better, he thought. Anna Andrews: Pamela's daughter. Between them, if you believed the hype, a formidable team.

'Good,' replied Wyles. 'If you can supply me with times, dates, places – that sort of thing. Oh yes, and photos.'

'Proof of Liaison,' replied Andrews.

'Sorry?' said Wyles, snapping his briefcase.

'It's called Proof of Liaison.'

'Er, yes,' said Wyles. 'You see, I'd, er, particularly like to know if any of them are co-habiting.'

Andrews flickered a slight smile. 'You're not DSS are you?'

'No, no,' said Wyles.'

In truth, Andrews had no problem with the DSS, rather favouring their secured transactions. But if Wyles was working for a government agency, she'd pass on the exes – all of them.

This certainly sounded an oddball case. Pry on seven couples? In her line of work she'd witnessed multiple suicides, multiple partners and even multiple orgasms. But multiple divorces?

But Wyles had absolutely no intention of elaborating. Simply find the fourteen, check relationships, report back.

Wyles hadn't wanted to use a private detective – or enquiry agent, or whatever – but doing it himself just wasn't an option. How could he fit snooping on fourteen people – spread around

London – into his schedule? He couldn't ask MediSee for help either. Data protection, medical practice, double-blind testing… it would break about a dozen laws. That's assuming they'd even know where they'd all copped off to. So that left doing nothing: putting out a press release suggesting that Pheroxosol could keep couples together with nothing to back that up.

But what if someone wanted proof – which, knowing the tabloids, they would. And what if, having made such an outrageous claim, the couples weren't even couples? How stupid would CalmerCeutical look then? No, they couldn't simply base their claims on what happened during the trials. After all, coupling up, when cooped up, was commonplace. So he was left with few choices. Enquiry agent or nothing. And nothing, given rewards, wasn't an option.

So, having Googled a few agencies, it was an easy decision. Not only did Andrews have all the right attributes – she was even a woman, for God's sake, far better at the lovey dovey stuff – but she was based in South East London too, which, given where the trials had been, was probably where most of the inmates would be. But he was from Slough – the other side of planet London.

Yet even that could be a plus. You see, the one thing he couldn't afford, was anyone at CalmerCeutical finding out. His science-brained colleagues, with neither the nose nor the nous for such things, would ridicule it.

The trials, till now, had gone like clockwork. All participants had shown better sleep patterns, lower stress levels and absolutely no ill affects. *And* they'd elected to continue with the medication after leaving the clinic.

Tedious work still lay ahead for MediSee though. Reports needed to be submitted to healthcare agencies and food and drug associations; further submissions would need to be made. And even after that, patent battles may need to be fought.

But all this testing, reporting and submitting could be worthwhile, *if* they hit the drugs jackpot. Which was precisely why Wyles had gone into pharmaceuticals in the first place.

And with a drug that could fulfill two functions – anti-depressant *and* anti-loneliness – he could double his chances. And because the latter tapped into people's innermost aspirations, the chances of Pherexosol being successful could multiply tenfold.

So for now, CalmerCeutical would continue to parade Pheroxosol as an anti-depressant – because that's what it was. But a few strategic hints at other benefits, assuming it *had* other benefits, certainly wouldn't go amiss – and a press release was top of that hint list.

There was nothing illegal in this. Quite the contrary. Wyles could justify these disclosures on a Best Financial Practice basis because, as a responsible CEO, he was *duty bound* to his shareholders to include any relevant information about potential new products. After all, company shares are sensitive to such information. So he had the shareholders best interests at heart. It just so happened that he was the biggest. Shareholder, that is.

Lily

You know, it's the simple words that say the most. Take '*and*' for instance. Sorry to go all TEFLy but it's just a conjunction. Just a word that's used to join two halves together. Two halves of a sentence, two halves of a story – maybe two halves of a life. Like Ben *and* Lily, for instance.

But if you stick '*and*' at the *front* of a sentence, which strictly speaking you shouldn't, it can be incredibly powerful. And if you start a whole story or a whole song with it, it's the missing stuff, the unsaid stuff that leaves you wondering.

For instance, let's take: '*And then he kissed me*'. What happened before? What happens afterwards? And how about: '*And now, the end is near…* 'That's brilliant! Starting a line about the *end* of something with the word 'and'. Then there's the opening line of the most powerful English song of all: '*And did those feet…*' Before those feet, what happened?

Well in my case, before those feet walked down that corridor, nothing happened. But afterwards, everything happened. Totally irresponsible. And just because I'm kicking off this story again from the point at which I can truthfully say: '*And then he kissed me*', it shouldn't have given me license to go off and have unprotected sex, should it? But it did. Or perhaps I should say: And it did.

I was lucky though. Lucky in the sense nothing nasty happened on the STD front, but also lucky in the sense that from then on, romantically, things began to flourish. However, in the days and weeks following that night, despite everything pointing to the contrary, my capacity to worry remained vast.

I've now got to the stage in life where I'm certain I'll always worry. Life could bestow upon me everything: love, wealth, health and happiness, and I'd still worry. In fact, they may be mutually dependent. Though that could just be a woman thing, of course.

But back to then and back to Ben.

In the days and weeks that followed the clinical trials, we fell deeply and hopelessly in love. Everything in our world became kind of in a glow, warm and floating. We'd walk along, literally, with our hands in each other's pockets – you know, arm-in-arm, but hands tucked into each other's jeans. We'd say little, smile a lot and look at each other with eyes like puppies in an Andrex commercial. I would imagine we were an embarrassment to everyone we encountered. But love is blind, and we just didn't care.

On the day the trials finished, we all had what we called our Escape Party at a pub nearby. It was good fun, in a glowing, floating, wholesome kind of way. And absolutely nothing like I would've guessed it would be like.

If you'd asked me at the beginning of the trials what a post-clinical party would be like, I'd have imagined it to be an evening of unrestrained drunkenness. After all, we'd got to know each other well, been confined to barracks, hadn't touched a drop of alcohol *and* it was a Friday. Perfect recipe for a party, I'd say.

However, the reality of that night was entirely different. Okay, we were jolly and happy, but certainly not in a raucous or crazy way.

And unless I was imagining things, everyone else was glowing and floating and smiley too. You see, rather peculiarly *everyone* seemed to be loved up. I know it sounds ridiculous, but it's true. There was Russ and Sophe, Johnny and Francine, Brendan and Vicky, Chris and Jasmine, Josh and Claudia and even Timmy and Tommy. And of course, there was us two: Mr and Mrs Lurve themselves. All smiling, all happy.

Anyone walking into that pub would have thought they'd walked into a Cliff Richard convention.

As the weeks and months went by, there were supposed to have been reunions. We had all promised ourselves meet-ups – where the girls could reminisce about the boys and the boys could reminisce about the farting – or whatever boys reminisce about. But it didn't happen. Oh yes, there was Facebook, but *real* gatherings need an organizer – someone to sort out venues and stuff. Now think about it. Have you ever asked someone in love to organize anything? Precisely. It was never, ever going to happen.

During those early weeks of freedom, Ben and I were living the dream – in all senses. Living in a dream as lovers, but living in a dream financially too. Ben's finances were collapsing. So together (we did everything together) we set about changing things. We cancelled expensive club memberships, stopped eating out and took buses instead of taxis. But there was one area of his lifestyle, the main component in fact, that wasn't so easy to rein back. His beautiful, airy, high-ceiling, sash-windowed Stoke Newington flat. Deep down though, and rather selfishly, I was pleased he couldn't sell it. You see, the main thing that flat had, apart from the high ceilings and the tall windows, was space. And compared to my little Lewisham bedsit, it was truly heaven on earth.

We didn't move in together, it was too early for that, but I did spend the weekends round there. And those weekends were wonderful – worth the working week, worth those metaphorical lengths of the corporation swimming pool. Yes, we had the occasional lover's tiff – one evening we disagreed about what he should wear to a job interview – but overall, our time together was pretty blissful.

Saturday mornings saw long lie-ins, a wander around Church Street, with it's pavement cafes, delis and antique shops; then, as the sun went down, a few drinks in the local pub and finally back to where we started – bed. Sundays meant even longer lie-ins, the Sunday Papers, walks around Clissold Park and even more bed. Monday mornings, of course, were back to reality – and work. It wasn't an easy journey either. A long walk, a bus, a train and a walk.

Ben was really sweet about this journey and used to travel with me on the first leg, taking the bus to London Bridge. Initially, this was because I didn't know the way, but on subsequent Mondays, when I really did know the way, he still came. I suppose he just wanted to be with me – God knows why, my Monday morning moods aren't great. But perhaps he also enjoyed sitting on the top deck of the bus. It was all a bit novel to him.

On occasions I also visited him mid-week, taking the train straight from work. Although the journey would have been impractical on regular basis, it did work quite well because it was effectively a reverse commute; traveling back into central London on relatively empty trains. I could even get my lesson plans done on the way, leaving me more time when I got to Ben's for other stuff!

One evening was different though. Instead of me traveling north, he traveled south.

Wednesday evening (after we'd done the other stuff) he took me to football. I'd never been to a football match before, so it threatened to be quite an experience. And we're not talking Arsenal or whatever – we're talking Millwall.

Now, I come from a totally non-football family. But even if Dad been a Match of the Day man, I'm sure he'd have been horrified to think I was going to the dreaded Den. I mean, they're all thugs aren't they? Actually, on consideration, I already had evidence that they weren't. Ben, for all his other faults, certainly wasn't that. In fact, when I once mentioned Millwall's reputation, he just laughed.

'Thugs? *Mugs*, more like,' he'd said.

'Why go then?'

'You don't choose your football team, Lily,' he'd said, shrugging over a pint. 'It's destiny. Like going bald or being gay.'

I'd smiled at this thought, but then Ben added: 'You can't just change your team.'

An interesting point. So in a man's world you can change your family but not your team. Tells you something, doesn't it?

Ben then thought for a few more seconds and said: 'In a way, being a Millwall supporter has made me a better person, anyway.'

'In what possible way, Ben, could being a Millwall supporter make you a better person?'

'Prejudice.'

'I don't follow?'

'Well, all you have to say is Millwall, and you're damned. Like telling someone you're a paedophile or something.'

'Why is that a good thing?'

'Because it makes you realize what it's like to be a minority. You know, to be Muslim or black or whatever.'

'So being a Millwall supporter is like being a Muslim?'

'Well,' he'd said. 'Just think about the song.'

'"No One Like Us",' I said.

'Exactly. Isn't that how every minority group feels?'

It was a fair point. Perhaps he was right. Except, from my limited knowledge of football, all supporters seems to believe they're victims. Where referees are concerned, at least. Isn't that the whole point? Anyway, the other half of that song goes: 'We Don't Care', doesn't it? And Ben *did* care – about a lot of things. Not, maybe, when we'd first met, but he did now.

You know, I don't think I'd known anyone change as much as him before. Unless it was me that'd changed. You know, less judgemental. Yes, maybe that was it.

The cost of the evening, at least, was zero. Ben still had a season ticket and was able to cadge Ned's (who was off partying somewhere) for me.

We took the short hop from London Bridge to South Bermondsey amongst hoards of others and it was little worse than any packed train out of London. They were mostly male, it's true, but some had kids and even wives, God forbid! Just like any football crowd, I suppose. Apparently, it was a big match for Millwall – a local derby against Crystal Palace and, as we were sucked ever nearer, crowds converged from all angles: a sea of backs and bobbing heads. Then I realized that Ben was doing something quite exceptional here. This was the place he went with his mates. This was the place he drank beer, discussed the game and did whatever blokes do. This was *not* the place where he held hands with girls.

In a way, even if he'd tried to, he could never have shown greater commitment than taking me to this place. But I didn't tell him that, of course.

When we finally entered the stadium, two tiers up, it almost took my breath away. By football standards, it's small – or so I'm told. But under the floodlights, it was a lake of colour – emerald green and blue, rimmed with dazzling, rooftop diamonds. Like some mother ship, sailing through the night air. Then I noticed that one end was all red and purple, not blue and white: the alien end. It was amazing. Sort of LS Lowry meets Brave New World.

Once it kicked off, the crowd became noisy or silent, animated or quiet, in unison – like some giant organism. And when Millwall did, eventually, score I found myself leaping to my feet and hugging Ben as if I'd been a believer all my life.

The goal prompted a final twenty minutes of mocking and counter-mocking with the red and purple hoards singing '*Sing when you're winning*' and the home crowd upping their own mocking anthem – a version of the old hit: '*For twenty-four years we've living next door to Palace – Palace, who the FUCK are Palace?*' which I must confess, I did found quite amusing.

I left the stadium arm-in-arm with Ben, elated and with the songs, both printable and unprintable, still ringing in my ears.

Who would have thought that little Lillian Blackstock, ex of the Beckenham Ballet School and ex-Head Girl of St Agnes's, Bickley, would find herself on the terraces singing songs like that? Love changes everything, I suppose.

Ben

Until Lily came along, I'd never loved anybody. Not my Mum, though that wasn't really her fault, nor my Dad, and that certainly was, nor any of the half-brothers or half-sisters who were scattered around the place, most of whom I'd never met. I didn't love Ned because he was my mate, and I didn't love any of the girls I'd copped off with – any more than they'd loved me. Pretty sad, but that's the way it was.

But Lily, I did love.

Was it a nice feeling? Well, that's not an easy question. It should be a straight 'yes' shouldn't it? I mean, to love and be loved is what the whole world wants. So yes, it was wonderful. But it was numbing too. Who wants to be permanently anaesthetized?

It was as if reality had been suspended (though that could also have been to do with being unemployed), to do with being a spare part for the first time in my life. And when you're unemployed, and when you're getting poorer and poorer, it colours, or perhaps discolours, everything you do. In love or not.

So love was lovely, Lily was lovely, but I was mixed up, too. And somehow the mixed up-ness of being out of work got mixed up with the mixed up-ness of being in love and the net result was... well, mixed up.

However, on the job front, suddenly, there was a sudden glimmer of hope. It was a Friday afternoon and I was looking forward to Lily coming round. You see, back in those days we spent the weekends together at my place. Anyway, at about four o'clock, out of the blue, Ned rang up. He said he'd heard about a vacancy that was coming up at an agency a friend of his worked at. I asked him what he knew about the place, and the work they do. He said it would fit me like a glove. And because I'd spent a few months out of work – lost some of my old swagger – I asked him what I should say, do and wear. You know, it's amazing how quickly you lose your confidence. He said I should just be my normal self, say my normal things and wear my normal stuff. In his words I was going to piss it. So to say he was bullish about my chances would be an understatement.

Despite that, I spent the next hour or so checking out their website and going over my CV, looking back at my showreel.

When Lily turned up, after a day's work and a difficult journey, she was worn out. Of course, I was full it. I kissed her, made her a cup of tea, curled up on the sofa with her and told her all about it. Though she's good talker, she's an even better listener – most girls are. So after she'd taken it all in, she had a few thoughts of her own – she wouldn't have been Lily without a few thoughts of her own!

She liked the minor changes I'd made to my CV and said my showreel looked brilliant. She was biased on that front, of course, and also conceded that she probably wasn't the best person to judge it. She also agreed with Ned that I should be my normal self at the interview. But she did differ on one big issue: Ned's idea of wearing my 'normal' clothes. On this, she had a strong point of view:

'Creative or not, you have to be smart.'

Now the thing that annoyed me about this was that she didn't know the industry like I did. Creatives dress casually. In fact, they can be downright scruffy.

Now, with regards to the strength of Lily's feelings on this, I was reminded of Ned's *other* point about women. I told you his theory about them instantly mutating into The Disapprovers, but he also reckoned they could just as easily and almost as quickly mutate into The Interferons. Well, maybe he was right. Lily just didn't understand advertising.

'If I dress up, they'll just think I'm being poncey,' I said, gesticulating. 'And, after all, I *do* know advertising, Lily.'

'I agree you know advertising,' she conceded. 'But even if the interviewer's wearing jeans and a tee shirt, they certainly won't think you're being poncey – quite the opposite.'

'I disagree. If the bloke opposite me is all scruffed up, and I'm tarted up in a suit, he'll just think I'm taking the piss!'

We were still on the sofa, but now markedly at opposite ends of it.

'I didn't say you should wear a suit. I just said you should be smart. And he certainly *won't* think you're taking the piss.'

Lily then went on, very calmly, to explain this thing she'd read about interview techniques. Apparently, according to this book, in some circumstances smartness was a *suppression* of seniority. 'And interviews are a prime example,' she said.

'Yeah, well,' I shrugged. 'That's books – I'm talking life.'

'Well, I'm only telling you what it said,' she said. 'Interviews aren't just about *you*, they're about the *interviewer* too.'

'*Obviously*,' I agreed.

'Well, the point is, if you wear smarter clothes than them, you're putting yourself *below* them.'

'How on earth do you work *that one* out?' I laughed.

'Okay,' she said. 'Let's turn it around. If you wear *scruffier* clothes, what are you doing?'

'Looking scruffier,' I replied.

'You know what I mean. If you wear scruffier clothes than the interviewer, you're putting yourself *above* them. Agreed?'

'No,' I said '*dis*agreed.' In the mood I was getting into, I'd have disagreed with her, whatever she'd said. But I must admit that I was beginning to see her point. And the next thing she came up with really *did* strike a chord.

'Take a formal thing – you know, a function,' she said, 'with dinner jackets and stuff. That's not to show status – it's the opposite – it puts everyone on a level playing field; and if some rock star or whatever turns up – in something scruffy – they're putting themselves *above* everyone, not below them.'

That was an amazing observation. You see, Ned and I had been to a fair number of sparkling do's – Cannes and stuff – where evening dress was *de rigueur* – and where most blokes *did* wear it. But we weren't most blokes. We were hotshots. So yes, even though we wore black, and even though we wore a tie, it was just as likely to be black drainpipes, sneakers and a leather jacket. Why? Well, if someone had asked us, we probably would have said it was because we were sticking two fingers up at convention – being rebels, or ironic – whatever. But thinking about it, she was right. We were putting ourselves *above* it. Being smartarses. So yes, she had a point. A bloody good one. But was I going to agree with her? Was I fuck!

You know, the strange thing about Lily, during those early months, was that I was beginning to understand her. Now you might not think that's strange at all. But believe me, up until her, I had never met a single woman I'd understood. Which brings me back to Ned's theories about women instantly turning into Disapprovers and Interferons.

I think he was right that, given half a chance, women do stick their oar in. Maybe they're hard-wired that way. But maybe there's a good reason for it. Women do seem to have mysteriously intuitive brains and also want to share them with everybody. But I suppose if you just have brief flings, intuitive brains are of no use. I mean, when you first meet a girl it's not advice you're looking for is it – some nugget of wisdom about how to shake someone's hand or not to fold your arms during an interview. That's not a lot of use when you're ripping each other's clothes off is it. Sensible advice during sex would be an absolute turn-off, wouldn't it?

You know, whatever happened to me during those two weeks at MediSee, it seems to have been truly life-changing. I was somehow developing a female brain – but as it was just a brain, I wasn't that bothered.

Maybe that's the point. Maybe when you're in love you become half of another person. Either way, it diffused that particular situation. Eventually, we agreed to differ and, after a couple of glasses of wine, a takeaway pizza and a circular stroll around Church Street, we ended up back to my place for lovely, uncomplicated sex – without advice.

A couple of days before the interview, I met up with Ned in town. I wanted to get his angle on things; any information could be useful. I intentionally made it *a couple of days* before the interview, just in case I fell back into my bad old ways and overdid the booze a little. Casual and informal may be good interview strategies in advertising, but being one hour late and stinking of booze certainly aren't.

We met up at The Crown & Two in Dean Street, and when I got there I was confronted by the same old scene: young guns, old boozers, people on the make. Ned was already standing at the bar.

'My man,' he said, clasping my hand, rather than shaking it – as is the way with us hipsters. He bought me a drink, and we spoke about work. His work, that is. Of course, this also brought up the subject of my *old* work. And according to him, his new partner; the guy that replaced me, was doing 'okay', but – as he slapped me on the shoulder – 'he'll never replace you, mate.'

Of course, this was bollocks. Everyone is replaceable, especially in advertising – and Ned was just being kind. But I still appreciated it. Strangely though, I no longer cared. If they'd offered me that job back – not that they would – I wouldn't have taken it. Mind you, the dosh would have come in handy.

We then moved onto the agency in general. Apparently they'd just won a big car account, but lost an equally big retail one – so beheadings and coronations all round. The memory of all that stuff: the hirings and firings, the knives in the back, came back like a chill down my spine. I wondered why I was considering getting back into that industry at all. But then I remembered. It's the money, stupid.

So this brought us round to the subject of my interview and, in Ned's considered opinion, I was going to 'absolutely piss all over them'. He then gave my shoulder a punch and added: 'They'll be sucking your dick, mate.'

As you can tell from this, he was fairly bullish about my chances – but the advice he gave me was the exact opposite advice of Lily's. Be cocksure, wear what you want, and kick their fucking arses.

As the evening wore on, we moved onto to other subjects. And as Ned became more pissed it became pretty clear that he didn't much care for Lily, or perhaps my relationship with her. And when he suggested that he and I go out that Saturday to some new bar in Shoreditch, I had to turn him down.

'Sorry Ned,' I said, 'I'm staying in on Saturday. We're off to her parents on Sunday, so I want an early-ish night. We'll probably just have a takeaway.'

'Her parents?' he said, shaking his head and looking down into his beer. 'You're fucking losing it, mate.'

'Well,' I shrugged, 'I promised I'd go. Anyway, it'll save some money.'

'Don't worry about that, I can sub you some fucking sovs – and anyway, you'll soon have stacks of cash.' He then downed another gulp of beer and added: 'We should be going out celebrating your new job.'

'I haven't got it yet, Ned,' I reminded him.

'You'll fucking get it, don't you worry about that.'

He slapped me on the back and went off for a piss, while I got in a couple more beers.

He was still doing up his flies as he came back through the gent's door, and noticeably swaying.

'I've been thinking,' he slurred, as he reached me. 'What's all this staying in bollocks?'

'What do you mean?' I asked, paying for the beer.

'Well, every fucking night you and her just stay in, don't you?'

'That's what you kind of do when you've got a girlfriend,' I said.

'Well why do they call it going out then?'

'What do you mean?'

'Well, everyone says, "I'm going out with such-and-such", but then they fucking stay in, don't they?'

He had a point, I suppose.

'They should call it staying in, not going out.'

Like I said, he did have a point.

The evening degenerated, but more for him than me, and that was about the last coherent thing he said. We said our goodbyes, with him off to Groucho's, me to Leicester Square Tube.

Going home on the underground, amongst the drunks and the semi-dead, I made a decision on the interview front. Okay, Ned was over the top, and, okay, he'd had a few drinks and was being bloke-ish. But he also knew advertising, as did I. And being in Soho, in the heart of it, made his opinions, sound right too. After all, everyone's brash and self-assured. So scruffy and cocky it would be.

Two days later, on a Friday, I turned up for the interview. I was dressed casually, though obviously not scruffily, in jeans and a tee shirt. When I was called in I tried to be as self-assured as I could get away with. And to me, the interview went okay, though perhaps not great. On the way out, I noticed a guy sitting in reception, exactly where I'd been sitting half an hour earlier. I couldn't say for sure that he was there for the next interview, but it was likely. What I can say though, is that he was wearing a suit. And even without a tie, he was ten times smarter than I was. Oh yes, and he was all of twenty-five. If he was there for an interview, I don't know if he got the job, but one thing I do know: I didn't.

One nil to women's intuition.

Lily

Over the next couple of months, we started to bring the other strands of our lives together. That's what relationships are, aren't they – lives joined. And you can't really join lives without meeting families and parents and stuff. I think it's girls who mostly lead the way on that front; I wouldn't mind betting that where parental introductions are concerned, most of them kick off with the girl's parents. Of course, it's not easy, but it has to be done. So that's what we did, one warm Sunday towards the end of May.

I had already laid down some ground rules with Mum and Dad. You do need rules when you're going into battle. I'd told Mum there was *no* need to clean the house from top to bottom, there was *no* need to spend the previous three weeks baking cakes and there was *no* need to spend two days trying on different outfits – thereby giving Dad loads of grief. I'd also told her to tell Dad that there was *no* necessity to have the lawn, the flowerbeds and his beloved vegetable patch looking like something out of *Gardener's World* – but of course, he could if he wanted to. But what I *mostly* didn't want was them making such a big deal that it ended up in a huge family row. Oh yes, and talking of family rows: Jenny, Steve and little Thomas were also going to be there. I was still furious at my sister for telling them about the clinical trials, so I didn't want all that coming up either. Via phone calls I'd got all that out of the way first, so everything was set up nicely.

The first thing I noticed, even before setting foot in the house, was that the net curtains were twitching at the front window.

It was about twelve o'clock when we arrived and I would imagine that Mum would have been at that window since eleven, at least.

She greeted me with a peck and a: 'Hello Lillian, are you okay?'

Now that's not a normal greeting. Not a 'Good to see you', or a 'You're looking well'. It's the kind of greeting you'd give someone who had been ill, suffered bereavement or, as in my case, had recently spent two weeks in hospital. And it was *precisely* the conversation I *didn't* want to have.

So I just answered, 'Yes Mum, why *shouldn't* I be?', effectively *daring* her to go down that 'I've been worried sick' road. Fortunately, for her, she didn't.

And seeing as she hadn't mentioned that there was a man standing on her doorstep, I added: 'And this is Ben, by the way.'

'Ah hello Ben,' she said. 'Would you like a cup of tea?'

Now that isn't necessarily an offer of a drink. It's an automatic response to anyone, apart from the postman and paperboy, who comes to the front door.

Having declined the offer, we then both stepped into the hall.

It became immediately apparent, before we'd taken off our jackets, that despite it being a stiflingly hot day, she'd turned on the central heating and cooked a huge Sunday roast. Bang goes the 'no big deal' rule. I didn't need to walk into the dining room and see the silver-plated cutlery and parallel napkins – or the crystal glasses and bottle of Mateus. As a kid, the smell of roast beef and Bisto was followed by *Alan Dell's Sounds Easy*, just as surely as day followed night. Captain's log, stardate: any Sunday in Beckenham.

Within a couple of minutes of being squeezed together on the sofa, there was a peep-peep outside as Jen and Steve arrived in their people carrier. It's a Renault, I think. Designed for a family of twenty-six. So that just left enough room for a driver, a passenger, plus strapped-in Thomas and accessories.

We all traipsed out to the front drive and shook hands and said hello's and stuff, and by now I was really beginning to feel sorry for poor Ben. There he was standing on a suburban driveway, on a baking hot day and in clothes he would never normally be seen dead in. He was even trying to hold a conversation with my Dad, Mr Mumble – who was muttering something along the lines of 'How's your job?', with Ben, rather awkwardly, replying that he was 'between assignments'. The thing that made me so cross about that was that I'd *clearly* told Dad about Ben's predicament, *precisely* to avoid the subject. But oh no, he just blundered straight in there. But I did know why Dad asked that question.

You see, Dad's more normal opening line would have been something like: 'What line of business are you in?' But he knew I'd already told him that – advertising – though he'd obviously forgotten. So he was trying hedge his bets by asking: 'How's your job?' That question covers the fact that he might, or might not, have already been told what Ben's actual profession was. It's a 'How's the family?' question – one you ask when you can't remember the children's names, the partner's name, or whether they are now divorced. You can still ask 'How's the family?' So Dad thought he was being dead clever with his 'How's your job?' but, as usual, he wasn't.

While poor Ben was standing there, looking down at his un-Ben-like shoes, my sister was bending my ears on the martyrdom of motherhood.

Why do we do it? Why do we have these ridiculous family get-togethers? My fault, I suppose. I suggested it – telling Ben to dress up as a Littlewoods catalogue because we'd had that difference of opinion about smartness.

After everyone had shaken everyone else's hand – on the front lawn like some kind of White House photo opportunity – we all traipsed back in to the house together with whinging Thomas and his three tons of toddler equipment.

We all sat down in the living room and Mum, yet again, asked if we'd like a cup of tea. This time, just to get rid of her, we took up the option.

Dad gave us all a thimble full of wine and we talked about anything that wasn't off limits. Off limits was anything to do with politics, religion or current affairs. Also to be avoided were references to Ben's non-job, how we met up and clinical trials in general. So it was fortunate that we all had little Thomas to talk about. And God, Jenny covered everything: teeth, potties, nappies, rashes, illnesses, sleeping, not sleeping, eating, not eating, things he could do (everything) and things he couldn't do (quantum physics). Don't get me wrong – I love Thomas. And he was at that 'pointing at things with stubby little fingers and talking gobbledygook' phase. But you can have too much of a good thing.

Fortunately, just as the food was ready to eat, Thomas was ready to sleep. Unfortunately, however, that meant Mum leaving the kitchen and filling the talk gap. And if anyone can fill a talk gap, Mum can.

She took off her pinny, sat at the table and got down to giving Ben a good grilling. Stuff like 'Where do you live?' – which I'd already told her – and, bizarrely: 'Do you play any musical instruments?', to which he replied: 'Only the mouth organ.' But it was when she moved onto: 'Have you had many girlfriends?', that I really narrowed my eyes at her. I mean, what was he supposed to answer? If he says yes he's a 'lady's man' (Mum's expression), if he says no he's a 'homo' (ditto). But it was the next question that really did it. Just after Ben had answered her 'girlfriends' question with a sensibly diplomatic 'just a few', she came back with 'And did *they* have dark hair?'

'Oh *Mum*,' I said, slamming down my fork. 'For *God's* sake.' To which she hurtfully replied: 'I was only trying to be polite, Lillian.'

She has always calls me Lillian at times like that.

Dad's the opposite. He is a man of few words and even fewer Lillian's. If he gets to a phone first – a very rare occurrence in itself – all you get back is: 'Oh hello', followed *maybe* by: 'How are you?', then: 'I'd best pass you over to Mum – she's right next to me', which she certainly would be, almost ripping the phone from his hand.

Jenny's main conversation piece had been put to sleep so she had little to say, though she was clearly fascinated by Ben.

I mean, he's quite good looking and I don't think she could quite believe I'd landed him. As for her hubby Steve, he had even less to say because he's in insurance.

When Thomas awoke, he threw tantrums and toys with equal ferocity and in the end Jen and Steve were forced to pack up and leave town.

We all stood on the drive again, kissed and waved goodbye and stuff, and promised to meet up again – as you do, but don't.

Then when we all traipsed back in Mum put her pinny back on and Dad fell asleep. And I suppose that was about it.

We finally left at about five; Dad, brutally awoken by Mum, instructed to drive us to the station. We declined though. The walk and the sanity would do us good.

As we sat in the Sunday train, gently clickety-clacketing home, I found myself thinking about Mum and Dad, regretting not being nicer to them. But we were never been that type of family. You know: touchy-feely and stuff.

I know they won't be around forever. They're already kind of fading – like a photo, or a newspaper left in the sun. Yet every time I see them for any length of time it all became too draining. So I become tetchy and argumentative, and it all ends with a barrier again. And, ironically, the only way to remove that barrier is to leave, regret and start all over again. So I go with intentions and leave with repentance.

I wish it wasn't like that. I wish I could show my feelings while I'm there.

Oh well, at least I had Ben. He had his eyes closed and I snuggled up. He'd been a star.

Ben

'Why don't you rent it out?' suggested Lily brightly, if matter-of-factly.

We were curled up on my sofa, watching Alan Sugar sack people with the sound turned down.

Her idea made sense; typical, female, logical. If I could rent out my flat I could use the money to cover my ever-spiraling mortgage. Great flat – maybe. Great part of town – definitely. But it was no longer affordable.

When I first moved in, it was like a dream. Like the ads I used to make: big rooms with sexy girls and hunky blokes in them – draped across this season's sofa. But not any more. No longer liberating. Debts seeping into every polished floorboard crevice. Yes, I still had the scattered cushions and the bare feet – and the adland rolled up trousers – but the whole thing was crushing me, depressing me. There are all kinds of technical terms for the position I was in: sub-prime this, negative-equity that. But I just favoured fucked. Totally and utterly.

'Yes, but where would I live?' I shrugged.

I could just about rent somewhere cheaper than my mortgage, but by the time I'd paid the agent's fees, there'd be nothing left. Back to square one.

She disentangled herself, reached for the TV remote and zapped it off. Then she turned to me, looked at me straight and said: 'Move in with McFlurry and me!'

And that's how the next stage started.

Within a couple of weeks, I'd put my flat in the hands of an agent – or at least, Lily had – and with a few suitcases full of stuff, moved from North London to South – and from my big airy apartment into her cramped little bedsit.

I have confession to make here – another confession: it was the very first time I'd ever lived with a girl. I suppose that's almost as sad as my earlier one – never having really loved anyone. Or perhaps the two just go hand-in-hand. Oh yes, it would be the first time I'd lived with a narrow-eyed, disapproving cat as well.

To say we were tight for space would be an understatement. A rickety bed, a gas stove and a curtained-off shower area were all we had. I suppose it could have been a perfect breeding ground for domestic discontent; for endless bickering and back-biting. But it wasn't. Maybe that was because it was so clichéd that we guarded against it. Our generation had been so bombarded with that stuff – from kitchen sinks, to sitcoms, to soaps – that we almost expected the problems before they happened.

God, there were enough of those bloke-leaves-toilet-seat-up scripts knocking about the agency. We had a couple of clients that just loved them. One was for a lager brand. They loved all that earthy, belching-in-underpants stuff. You know, the girl is soaking in a bath surrounded by Jo Malone candles and the bloke crashes in and farts. But that certainly wasn't us. We had neither a bath for Lily to burn candles around – and me to fart in – nor a toilet seat to leave up.

But clichés apart, living with a girl *was* a bit mystifying. It was the silly little things that surprised me most. Like going into the shower with a Speedo hat on. That's Lily, not me. Or the giant crocodile-jaw thingies – like the things you clamp onto a car battery to jump start it – for her hair. Then she'd spend hours blasting hot air into her ears – at exactly the same she was giving me some essential information.

You know, back at the agency, there were only two girlie goods that blokes wouldn't touch – feminine hygiene and hair products. Both ends were a mystery. So before I even moved in, I made a pact with myself. Vaginas and hair, like politics and religion, were out of bounds.

Discussion-wise only, of course.

Lily

I was a little worried about the idea of us living together, though it was something I'd been thinking about for some time. You see, living apart we'd been getting on so well. And I didn't want to spoil things. But I was also worried about Ben's financial situation. Not so much the money, that was never important to me, but the effect it was having on him. I think, for blokes, unemployment isn't just a financial thing, it's a self-esteem thing. Obviously it's that for women too, but we have two functions in life, they have just the one.

I knew he'd get work eventually, he was too good not to, but in the meantime he was piling up debt. And the other problem was that *he didn't* think he'd get work. And it's what people think about themselves that counts.

According to his contacts in the business, the recession in the high streets was now affecting advertising severely. I encouraged him, of course; told him not to worry, that jobs would still come up and it was just a matter of time. But he wouldn't run with it and the situation was visibly wearing him down.

So during mid-week evenings, when Ben and I were apart, I found myself picturing my little hovel with us in it – plus McFlurry, of course. If it were possible, he could let his place out, pay the mortgage and then go back to his big beautiful flat once he found work.

Actually, in my heart of hearts, I was also hoping that one day *we* could go back to his big beautiful flat, but perhaps that was just make-believe.

In the mean time, would my place be too cramped? Would we fight? Like I said, I had my doubts. After all, relationship-wise, if it ain't broke, why fix it — we were getting along just fine. But Ben *was* broke, so financially speaking, he *did* need fixing.

One evening, when we were round at his place, I braced myself and brought the subject up. And after some thought, he went for it. He had far less problem with it than I'd expected — less than me, probably. And two weeks later, on a wet Saturday, I helped him haul suitcases across London and finally there we were: two peas in this very small pod.

I'd never really lived with a man before, unless you include when I was back at uni, where Adam and I spent so much time in each other's company that we might as well have been. Actually, what with the cramped conditions and the shoestring budget, there were similarities. But that's all they were, similarities. When you're a student, it's not just your room that's small, it's your world — the campus, the lecture rooms, the finite period of time. This was the real world. This was working week for me and job hunting for him — plus shopping and washing and getting on with life. And surprisingly, we coped very well.

I suppose we were lucky that it was at the beginning of summer. With the days being long and the weather mostly reasonable, we spent our evening walking, talking and sometimes just dreaming. On one occasion we even danced! You see, Lewisham's shopping precinct is all closed off at night, except for one area which allows access to a couple of bars which stay open longer. We'd had a drink in one of them and were wandering back to the flat through the empty precinct. The background muzak was still playing so we struck up a slow, smoochy dance together. Suddenly, an echoing voice came over the Tannoy came: 'Nil points.' We hadn't allowed for the security cameras. So we did a bow and, from the faceless watcher, got a round of applause — then continuing on our way, like giggling, love-struck kids. It was only a tiny incident but it somehow summed it all up. Back then, life was a waltz.

In truth, my flat wasn't really big enough for two people and a large, territorial cat. But somehow it seemed to work. Maybe when you're happy you don't need much space, or maybe we were both just determined to make it work.

From Ben's perspective, he was under less pressure, which helped. His flat was very quickly let and the money coming in was slightly more than his mortgage; so he even had a small income. And I suppose that way of looking at things – the turning of problems into answers – was the way we dealt with that whole episode. McFlurry, being the whore he is, now had two kneading laps and could play one person off against another. As for Ben, he was quite literally living out of a suitcase – there hardly being enough draw space for one, let alone two. And it's a fine line. If we'd let our stuff get all mixed up – shirts, socks, bras and knickers – it may have ended up in arguments. But if we'd been too obsessive about space and neatness – demarcation lines and stuff – that too would have been a minefield. So it just needed balance, and balanced we both were. Maybe it was the medication. We were still both taking our free supplies and, in theory, that was supposed to keep you on an even keel.

So McFlurry and Ben were fine, but what of me? Did I miss my independence? Not really. If anything, his presence made things cosier. For instance, with such a tiny bed, it solved the problem of who slept on which side because we both sort of fitted together like a pair of curled-up, pink prawns. And after all, with just a single space performing so many functions, how many couples can say they've had sex in the bedroom, the lounge, the dining room *and* the kitchen all in the same night!

But on that subject – well, sort of – there was just this one thing. One thing that was *really* beginning to worry me.

The Meeting Room

'It needs to be clearer,' said Wyles, gesturing towards the press release lying in front of him. 'You know, more to the point.'

Amraj and Samuel looked doubtfully down at their own copies. As far as they were concerned, it was pretty much par for the course. It kicked off with '*About the Trials*', an introduction giving the where's, when's, and how's. This was followed by a section called '*About Pherexosol*', which covered the what's and what for's. And finally there were a few paragraphs entitled '*About CalmerCeutical*', which filled in the who.

It was designed to be read by both scientists and money men; therefore it included some pharma-speak, such as 'double-blind' and 'un-subcutaneous dosing', but also included financial jargon such as 'investment opportunities', 'going forwards' and 'revenue streams'.

Amraj's job had simply been to cut and paste Dr Taylor's report on patient's responses and improved sleeping patterns, plus add some extra bits and pieces. Samuel, with an eye on the marketing, had added some sexy bits for the City and some colour photos. Frankly, it was standard stuff.

'We need a stronger reference to the whole emotional thing,' said Wyles.

'Emotional thing?' replied Amraj.

'Yes. We've been over this a hundred times – that whole *luurve* thing.'

Wyles found it necessary to make fun of the word 'love'. This could have been because they were scientific men, discussing a scientific subject. More likely though, it was because it wasn't a word he felt comfortable with. Either way, it did the trick. His colleagues knew exactly what he was talking about – yet were also able to share the gag.

'Oh right, *luurve*,' concurred Samuel. 'We could add a few lines to the fourth paragraph, I suppose. We've already put something in there about people getting on well.' He then picked up the release, scanned it and added: 'That's it: "*The participants showed higher than usual levels of interaction.*" Then he shrugged: 'I suppose we could change it to: "*The participants showed higher than usual levels of luurve.*"'

This failed to get even a smile from Wyles, and when Amraj rather undiplomatically suggested that he couldn't see much wrong with the original wording, his boss nearly hit the roof: '"*Higher levels of interaction*"! – *Higher fucking levels of interaction!* Fucking namby pamby stuff! We need something with bollocks!'

'It was, er, roughly what Dr Taylor put in his report,' suggested Amraj.

'I don't give a shit about Dr Taylor. He's not responsible to shareholders – I am. We need something that'll whip up a bit of interest.'

'But we can't make claims we can't substantiate, Will,' said Samuel.

Amraj backed this up: 'We'd need different trials, Will. Different numbers.'

'Precisely,' said Wyles, calming down a little. 'We'd need to do different trials.'

'Sorry,' frowned Amraj, confused that his boss was now agreeing with them. 'Are you saying we should do further tests?'

'Not immediately no, these things need funding. But if we're going to go forward with this – this whole 'luurve' thing – we need to generate interest.'

'So how do you propose, er, we put it?' asked Samuel, looking back down at the document.

With palms down on the table, Wyles separated two sheets of A4 and slid them across the table – one to Samuel, one to Amraj.

'Most of what you've written is fine. I'd just like to add this paragraph.'

They took a few seconds to take it in, but it was Samuel who looked up first, a little stunned. 'I'm er, not sure we can put this in, Will.'

'Why not?'

'Well, I mean…'

Stuck for words, Samuel simply read straight from the page: "*More stable relationships could also be a byproduct of this research. At the time of writing, some three months after the completion of the trials, almost 75% of the participants were maintaining romantic links that had been initiated during the trials.*"

He looked back up at his boss and said: 'Um, don't you think that it's a little… well, um… ' he let his sentence trail off.

But if he was expecting a response from his boss, it wasn't forthcoming. He got support from Amraj, though: 'Sorry Will, but where did you get these figures from? I mean "*almost 75%*"? And how do we know they're "*maintaining romantic links*"?'

At this point Wyles didn't answer; merely putting the paper back down and looking up at his two employees. He knew this question would come, but didn't really have a plan. He could have shown them the photos from The Andrews Agency, which sat in a large brown envelope in front of him. And from that same envelope, he could also have then taken out Pamela Andrew's report. But in the end he did neither. When it came to the imparting of information to his employees, he favoured the 'need to know' system. And they needed to know nothing.

'Trust me, Amraj. Of the original group of fourteen… that's seven couples,' he held up the fingers to prove it, 'eight are definitely seeing each other on a very regular basis. And of the remainder, two are currently on holiday – almost certainly together. So only four – *yes four* – are definitely *not* together – *all* of whom *already* had long-standing relationships.' He looked at them full in the face and added: 'You could almost argue 100%.'

This silenced his employees, partly because it was pretty impressive, but also because it was so detailed.

Wyles was determined to ram it home though: 'And the point is, none of them – *none of them* – knew each other before these trials started.'

Satisfied with his argument, he then leaned back and gave a parting volley: 'Now I'd say that was worth a shout, wouldn't you?'

They were dumbfounded. It was indeed worth a shout. But it did raise a rather obvious question. And it was Samuel who cleared his throat and ventured it: 'Um, sorry Will, but how can you be so... what I mean is, how do you *know* all this?'

'I just do,' he shrugged. 'Just like I knew that Pearson's were trying to poach Nick, and Tomlinson was shagging Amanda. I'm your CEO. I *know*.'

Ben

At that particular point in my life, I was finding it difficult to pinpoint exactly why I was going through such big changes. I mean, I was in my thirties, hardly male menopausal or anything. On top of which, the changes I'm talking about aren't that sort – almost the opposite, in fact.

All of a sudden, I was more contended, sleeping well (and I wasn't used to sleeping with females either – in the literal sense), not fancying everything in a skirt (except Lily, that is) and hardly drinking a drop. Obviously Lily was a factor in all this, but certainly not in any nagging, hectoring sense.

It could still have just been down to female influence, I suppose. You know, simply being around all those fluffy, pink hormones. But if it was, it was certainly bloody subtle. Then again, I can almost hear Ned's answer to that: 'But women *are* bloody subtle, Ben.'

So if it *wasn't* just Lily, what else could it have been? Well, maybe it was not being in advertising. There's no doubting it, that job supplied the means: silly money, endless jollies, sleepless nights, loads of stress – making me drink even more. The whole vicious circle thing.

But *un*employment is stressful too. And so is the living out of a suitcase. And so is being poor. So if I was looking for another circle that was equally vicious, it was sitting there in that tiny flat, tempting me, practically blowing fucking kisses at me. Surely, if anything could put me back on a boozy, unhealthy lifestyle, that could.

I had made conscious efforts to be constructive too. The first thing I'd tried was swimming. Now that *was* Lily's influence because she really loved it. She used it as a metaphor for life, ploughing up and down, manfully – if that's the right word – through the swimming lanes of life. We went together at first, but she went off at twice the speed I could, with three times the elegance – leaving me thrashing around amateurishly in her wake. I also went a few times by myself, but I didn't really like it. Too wet for a start.

So I tried meditation. Which was certainly drier. But in a way, it was tougher too. You know, I don't think humans are designed to do nothing. Mentally, I mean. With the possible exception of Dad who, according to Mum, made an art form out of it.

Me, I needed something more physical. So one day I put on my tracksuit bottoms, a tee shirt, and trainers and, as the old song goes, found what I was looking for. My little Everest.

Above our tiny flat (notice the 'our'), rising in gentle steps from the back of Lewisham High Street, is Hilly Fields. From a distance (if the tower blocks weren't in the way) it's like a layer cake made of terraced houses and trees, with a park stuck on the top. Or a bit like a bald bloke with semi-detached hair. Okay, it's no mountain, but it's not flat either.

I started by walking up the hill and then jogging round the park at the top. Then, as I got fitter, I started to jog the downward stretch too. That was easy. Finally, in longer and longer chunks, I joined it all together.

I achieved that goal by late June and the feeling – once I arrived at the top, with sun caressing and endorphins swirling – was magnificent.

Sometimes I'd pause up there, partly because I was knackered but mainly because of the views. There I'd pant, hands on hips, just looking. To the east, across Lewisham's sprawl, was a backdrop that was almost Lancashire mill town – Lowryesque and gritty. And to the west, rising out of a distant hill, was Crystal Palace – a sort of poor man's Eiffel.

And as I stood there, getting my breath back and feeling good – if a little knackered, I made a pact with myself. If I ever got back into advertising – which I kind of had to, really – then running would be my drug of choice.

Perhaps I had a natural affinity with this area too; after all, I was born a south Londoner. So the other thing I decided, as I scanned that landscape, was that I should contact Mum; her little flat was out there somewhere. Maybe Dad too – though *not* with Mum, that's for sure.

So after I'd jogged down the hill one day, I rang her. She was dead pleased to hear from me. Pleased I had a steady girlfriend too, and that I was living locally. Obviously the news about work wasn't so good, but being unemployed is pretty much a family tradition, so I don't think it worried her too much. She even asked us round that very evening. So I said yeah, of course, why not.

After I'd put the phone down I decided to do a bit of job searching. I was one of my regular afternoon activities – head in laptop, mouse in hand – searching advertising websites. It was then that I stumbled across a real surprise. Actually, it was more than just a surprise it was an absolute 24-carat shocker.

You see, as there didn't seem to be any jobs in the offing (surprise, surprise), I thought I'd check out clinical trials. Perhaps I could earn a couple of grand that way again. I couldn't remember the name of the clinic, but I certainly could remember was the name of the drug – after all, I took it every day – so I put Pherexosol into Google and about half a dozen entries came up. No particular surprise there. And four down was the very name I was looking for: MediSee. So I checked them out and yes, they did have some vacancies coming up. I made a note of the dates and quit back to Google.

Then, for no particular reason, I clicked into one of the other entries for Pherexosol – a company called CalmerCeutical. I opened it up and it became immediately obvious that they were the people that made the stuff.

I was just going to quit entirely when I read '... *and the majority of participants showed a greater predisposition towards the initiation and maintenance of romantic partnerships.*'

I read it. Then re-read it. Then re-read it again. And unless I was misunderstanding what it was saying, it suggested that the people who took part in the trials – you know who – were more likely to cop off with each other *and* stay together afterwards!

So I went back into Google and opened up some of the other entries for Pherexosol. One was from *The Financial Times* and, amongst other things it said: '*UK pharmaceutical company CalmerCeutical, are researching the possibility that Pherexosol, their new drug, could encourage greater stability in human relationships - particularly those of a romantic nature.*' Same thing, slightly different wording.

Next, I opened up an entry from *New Scientist*. This was far bigger and far more detailed, and contained all sorts of stuff about things like dopamine and oxytocin. But again, halfway down: '*Research in both rodents and humans suggest that this drug could encourage more monogamous relationships*', and again, further on, an almost identical entry to the others: '*... could be instrumental in stimulating and maintaining romantic partnerships*'.

Jesus! Perhaps some of the changes I'd been going through were a little easier to explain than I'd imagined!

Lily

'I think I'm pregnant,' I said, feeling my chin wobbling. You see, Suzie was the first person I'd told.

She put her coffee down, moved along the sofa and flung her arms around me. I immediately broke into a flood of tears: inconsolable, salty, self-pitying. Something I'd been determined not to do.

I'd thought about telling Ben first, of course. But after I'd agonized and agonized, and changed my mind a million times, I decided against it. That's what best friends are for, I thought. And Suzie was my best friend – perhaps my *only* friend.

I had begun to have a few inklings even before my period was due. It was just a few silly things, like sore boobs and perhaps a bit of female intuition. I kind of put it to the back of my mind; after all, I'd only just started back on the pill so my body hadn't settled into much of a rhythm. But two weeks after it was due, still nothing. I started to have more genuine worries. I left it a couple more weeks then decided there was only one course of action. I bought a tester from Boots, followed the instructions, steeled myself, and waited the prescribed two minutes. Bang, there it was. Clear as day. Or blue as day, because that's the colour the line's supposed to be. Or *not* supposed to be, depending on your point of view.

And what *was* my point of view? Well, to put it mildly, I was confused.

In a way, you could argue that it was perfect timing. I was thirty and Ben thirty-two. Ideal ages, you could say. And after all, he was the nearest thing I'd ever had to a proper partner – better than many people's, I'd guess – and would probably make a good father too. So why not just tell him? After all, he'd probably be delighted. Where's the problem?

Well, here's the problem – or *problems*. Number one: by normal standards, we'd only just met. Number two: we'd never discussed marriage, or babies or even living together – like the pregnancy itself, the co-habitation had just been luck: good or bad. Number three: money. I was earning almost nothing, which was slightly better than Ben, who was earning *exactly* nothing. Number four: accommodation. We lived in a one-bedroom shoe-box. Number five (and perhaps you could call this number one): I just didn't feel ready.

And they were just the actual facts. When you start adding the 'what ifs' it becomes an avalanche of doubt. What if Ben walks? He wouldn't be the first bloke to do such a thing; and would I really want to bring up a baby by myself? What if Ben doesn't walk, but only stays because he feels he *mustn't* walk? Is that the kind of life I want? What if I don't love the baby because I end up blaming it for pulling my life to pieces? Once you added that lot to the lack of money, the one-roomed bedsit and the feeling of not being ready, well, the word termination comes to mind. Let me repeat that word in all its starkness: termination.

But I wasn't certain I wanted that either. You see, I'd always wanted kids – couldn't imagine going through my life without them. And, as I mentioned before, thirty is about the best age. And after all, I may never get another chance. That's a complete reverse type of 'what if'. What if I have an abortion, and quite apart from the pain and guilt that will bring, I never meet anyone else? What if I went through all that and ended up bitter, old and lonely? God, I was mixed up. Which was why I hurried round to Suzie's.

After she'd finished hugging me and patting me, she took my coat, sat me back on the sofa and, as I dabbed at my last few big sobs, said: 'I'd offer you a wine, but I suppose you shouldn't.'

'No', I said, 'but I'd love a tea.'

A little falteringly, I set about explaining the whole thing to her; how I wasn't on the pill when we met and how, stupidly, the first few times we had sex it was unprotected and after that it was simply down a combination of condoms, hope and trust in Ben. Since then I'd got better organized, but horses and stable doors come to mind.

Suzie's sister had just had a baby, so she gave me lots of practical advice: take it easy, stay off the drink, go to the doctor – all the obvious stuff. She also said one thing I hadn't thought of though: be careful with medication – *any* medication. I suddenly remembered the Pherexosol. I only had about three weeks supply left so that would go straight in the bin.

She said lots of kind words too, of course. She said that whichever way I went, whatever I wanted to do, she'd be there for me. Of course, that begged the obvious question. What *did* I want to do? Did I want it?

Well, if Ben wanted it, I wanted it, I told her. And if Ben didn't, then I wasn't so sure. Not so sure at all.

'There's only one way to find out,' she said, clutching my hand. 'You've got to tell him.'

I thought for a second.

'And what happens if, you know,' I found myself starting to sob again, 'if it turns him against me?' I dropped my head: 'What happens if he – if he leaves?' I could feel the tears welling up. 'You see, Suzie, he's the best thing I've ever…'

She lifted my chin back up, looked at me straight in the tearful eyes and said: 'Then if he does that, Lily, he's *not* the best thing you've ever had – he's a shit.'

She was right, of course. Best friends generally are.

He had to be told.

Ben

I agonized for ages. Sitting there, looking at the packet, wondering whether my whole relationship – *our* whole relationship – simply came down to this. All those feelings, all the stuff I'd never felt for anybody before, just down to chemicals.

After much thinking and Googling and re-thinking… and after deciding to tell Lily and then deciding not to tell Lily, I made up my mind.

If nothing else, the one thing I *was* going to do was to *stop* taking it. That way I could see if it was true. See if it affected our relationship – or at least, my half of our relationship. You see, I just had to know. And if it did affect my feeling towards Lily, I had a choice. I could live with my new feeling for her – and suffer whatever consequences that threw up. Or, if I *couldn't* live with those consequences, I could simply start taking the medication again. Simple. My bigger dilemma was with Lily though. Should I or shouldn't I tell her?

Up until then, as far as I knew, there had been absolutely no secrets between us. I kept nothing from her and she kept nothing from me. But after much thought, I decided this was going to be the first. I wasn't going to tell her. Okay, if she found out herself, as I had done, that would be different. But why force it? Why not simply try the experiment on myself first?

You see, if I did tell her, she might find herself imagining, believing, that her feelings were all down to the drugs – even if they weren't. That might happen to me too, of course. But the difference for me was the genie was already out of the bottle, so to speak – I couldn't *un*know what I already knew. Couldn't simply *un*read what I'd just read. Lily wasn't in that position, and her ignorance could also be her bliss. Anyway, like I said earlier, for me, I could start taking it again whenever I wanted, and no one would be any the wiser.

And my clinching argument, the one that finally persuaded me to keep quiet about it, went like this: One of us keeps taking it (Lily) and one doesn't (me). That way it would be easier to find out what effect, if any, it was actually having. Well, that was my logic anyway.

Oh yes, and one other thing I was going to do was to contact MediSee. They had absolutely no right peddling stuff with known side effects. Okay, in this case, they were nice side effects. But nice or not, it should be our choice, not theirs.

When Lily came home I told her about my idea of visiting Mum and she said: 'Yes. Good idea.' I suppose, like most women, she liked the idea of happy families. And that's fair enough because they're certainly better than unhappy ones, aren't they? But when I said I was going to visit her *that evening*, she said I should have given her more warning and that she was too tired. Now I could certainly understand the 'too tired' – she'd just got back from work – but not so much the 'more warning' bit.

'More warning for what?' I asked.

That didn't go down too well. I guess needing warning is a bit of a female thing.

But once she'd sat on the sofa for a while, had a cup of tea and told me about work, she got up and started sifting through drawers and pulling faces into mirrors and stuff. So it looked as though she might be up for it after all. I wasn't absolutely certain though, so I asked her, sort of tentatively: 'We are still going, then?'

I didn't really get an answer, so I kept my head down for a bit and watched telly. She still seemed less than happy about the idea, but equally wasn't settling down for a night in either.

And whatever she was getting ready for – I assume it was to go to Mum's – she was still pretty fretful about it; sitting on the bed, pulling things on, sighing deeply, taking them off again.

Thinking about it, I suppose the idea of meeting someone's mum – even my silly mum – could stress you out a bit. Especially after a day's work.

So I said to her: 'Tell you what Lil, it's really no problem, I'll go by myself.'

But she didn't like that idea either, saying it would make her look bad.

So I said: 'Right, no problem, I'll just cancel.'

I picked up my mobile to dial Mum's but Lily said: 'No, I am coming, but just don't hassle me.'

I took a big intake of breath, counted to ten and went back to the telly.

After another half hour, she was still pulling things out of wardrobes, so I told her not to worry too much about clothes: 'Mum never does.'

'So I gather,' she replied, caustically.

Now although Lily had never met Mum, I'd told her all about Mum's dress sense – or perhaps undress sense. Now Lily is a very sharp girl and that answer did show it; quite clever, really. But it was so un-Lily-like. Said with too much venom.

'Look,' I said, 'is there something wrong?'

'No,' she said. 'Apart from the fact that I've only just come back from work and now we've got to visit your mother.'

Notice the 'mother'. Not mum. A few seconds earlier she was implying she was some kind of slag, which I didn't actually mind, because she was – once. But suddenly it's *mother*.

Clearly this could have turned into a major row – maybe it already was – and I could have called it all off there and then. But that would have solved nothing because whether we now did or didn't go, the row was set to simmer on all night. So in the end I just kept my mouth shut and my head down and just waited for the storm to blow over. But one way or another she was determined to have her pound of flesh out of the 'no warning' issue – *and* to martyr it out.

By the time we'd bought some rather crap flowers round at the service station, missing a bus in the process, we were running about three-quarters of an hour late; so I too was getting stressed, and beginning to wish I'd never thought of it. There again, I hadn't seen Mum for ages. In fact, I'd never even been to her new flat. I suppose that sounds a bit negligent, but in my defense, she'd only recently moved there, and I had visited her in every other ruddy flat she'd had. And my God, she'd had plenty. Come to think of it, she'd had plenty of everything: blokes, fights and babies. Life of plenty, I suppose. Apart from money, that is.

After we got off the bus, I got my bearings and then led Lily through some rather depressing backstreets. By now, I was really regretting the whole thing. Mood-wise, stress-wise and location-wise. We were in the middle of a brutal, graffiti-daubed council estate and the only signs of life were the occasional white hoody, black gangsta, or pit bull.

Mercifully, by the time we got to Mum's, things had begun to look up – lower-rise housing, fewer window bars and almost daub-free. And once we'd climbed the single flight of steps there was even a potted geranium outside her door – though it did have fag butts pushed into it.

After a showy doorbell, an instantly turned-down TV and some familiar hair titivating behind the rippled glass, Mum appeared.

''Ello Ducks,' she said, giving me a minty kiss (mouth-freshener, good sign; she cared).

'And you must be Lily,' she added, giving her a peck too.

Lily gave Mum the flowers, Mum said they were lovely – which they weren't – and we all went inside.

Although the flat wasn't familiar, most of the contents certainly were. We were shown to a mustard-coloured sofa that I'd done battle with before; heaving it down the steps of one of her previous abodes after one particularly acrimonious eviction. And to the right of us, like some museum exhibit, was a glass cabinet containing fancy gold-rimmed wine glasses, a lead crystal decanter and a silver salver nutcracker set that

I could picture from Christmases past. Every year they would appear, together with the gin bottles, 'Eat Me' dates and Slade albums.

Also recognizable was a nest of occasional tables that I used to figure-eight my Scalextrick around – upon which was a glass Martini ashtray; a veteran of a thousand stubbings but still in surprisingly good nick. It had probably outlived many of its stubbers.

Mum asked us if we'd like a cuppa 'or something stronger'. We went for the cuppa, hoping that Mum would too. No chance. As ever, she went for the something stronger.

She went out to brew up, leaving us together on the sofa. I noticed that Lilly was seated a little too upright and, rather awkwardly, had her hands placed on her knees. Quite obviously she was finding the evening pretty tough.

She was peering at the many photos dotted around the walls, so I pointed out some: half-brothers, quarter-cousins, unknown uncles. But in many cases, even though I didn't recognize the images, I was familiar with the frames. Oh yes, and no Dad. Like photo, like man. I knew, before we arrived, there'd be one of me somewhere – gappy-teeth, squiffy tie, mottled-grey background. And I'd imagined what Lily would say when she saw it – the laughter and the teasing. But as it turned out, when I pointed it out, she seemed a little apathetic. All I got back was: 'Oh yes, I can see the likeness.'

What was wrong with her? Okay, we'd had a row. But this wasn't the Lily I knew. She almost seemed as if she was somewhere else.

'That's yer boy,' said Mum, returning with sausage rolls, things in dips, peanuts and crisps – despite telling her not to go to any bother.

'Right little terror,' she said, unloading the tray.

'I bet he was, Mrs Dryden,' replied Lily.

At that point, I froze. My Mum isn't a Dryden, she's a Roberts. The only reason I had stuck with Dryden was because it's what I've got on my birth certificate. It was stupid of me to forget to tell Lily, but somehow it just never crossed my mind.

Credit to Mum though, she just said: 'Oh just call me Kath,' and moved on.

It occurred to me that it was a situation that had probably arisen before. You see, I've got some half-brothers and sisters called Petrov and some others called O'Donnel; and their partners may well have made the same mistake. What a mess of a life. I made up my mind, there and then, that if I ever had kids it would never happen to me. To have your children named after someone you really hate must be awful.

The conversation was okay, but not great. And although the evening didn't progress especially well, at least it progressed. I don't think Mum really noticed that Lily was cooler than normal though. After all, she'd never met her before, so how would she know? As for Mum, as long as she had someone to listen to her endless stories about the past, she was happy. Mind you, the huge Bacardi's helped, too.

About nine-thirty, we left; on Mum's advice we went back the other way through the estate. It wasn't quite so bad – well, not in a life-threatening way, anyway. You know, there was this thing that one of the partners at the advertising agency once said to me: '*When I was young, I thought money was everything...*' He'd paused before adding: '*But now I'm old, I realize that... it's true.*'

I didn't mind being unemployed and poor at thirty-odd, but I was fucked if I was going to be like Mum at sixty.

Also, all my kids would have the same surname.

Lily

'Good news, Lil,' said Ben, as I wearily pushed my way through the front door.

It was good to see him in such a buoyant mood. For what I was about to tell him, he'd need to be.

'I did try your mobile, but I couldn't get through,' he said, giving me a kiss.

'Oh, yeah, I'm sorry. I switched it off in class and must've forgotten,' I said, putting my bags down and slumping onto the sofa. 'So what's the big news?'

'I've got an interview – a really good one.'

'Well done,' I replied, and I meant it. Not only was that good news indeed, but his timing may yet turn out to be impeccable.

He made me a tea and told me all about it. Apparently, he'd been contacted by someone who he used to work with at his old place. This bloke had set up a 'shit-hot digital agency' which was, according to Ben, 'the way advertising's going'. And unlike the previous places he'd been for interviews, this was a person he 'really, really wanted to work for'. The post was Senior Creative – a step up from what he'd done before – and the clients were 'really, really A-list'.

'It's not just money,' he said, adding that he didn't know the exact figures, but that they would be, according to this friend 'substantial'. Substantial sounded good. Substantially better than nothing, anyway. Ben then said that if he could pull some business from his old place, 'the sky's the limit'.

It was good to see him so happy and positive – certainly a contrast to the night before. For the first time, we'd slept separately.

Actually, I need to qualify that. *He'd* slept separately – on the sofa – I'd slept in the bed. *My* bed.

We'd had this row about visiting his mum. I didn't have a problem with that, per se – in fact I really wanted to meet her. The problem was that the daft sod just dropped it on me – you know, the way blokes do. They just *don't* think. And what with everything else, I really could have done without it. But I went along with it and visited her, but when we got back home it all kicked off – he asked me why I was so morose at his mum's and I told him it was because I was bloody knackered, adding: 'Unlike you Ben, *I've* done a day's bloody work,' which was a cheap shot. So anyway, after a couple more even cheaper shots, I got the bed and he got the sofa.

Actually, as it turned out, it saved him twenty-four hours of worry. After all, if it hadn't been for that row, I probably would have told my news. So for him, ignorance was bliss. For a day, anyway.

I took off my working clothes, put on some comfortable jeans and a sweater, went to the bathroom, looked at my face – I looked tired and drawn – went back into the lounge and sat down on the sofa again. Ben was next to me, deep into his laptop, doubtless going over this new company's web page. I decided now was the time. He needed to know.

'The interview's on Monday,' he said, before I had a chance to say my well-rehearsed piece.

'Oh right, that's good,' I said, leaving it a beat before going for it: 'Um Ben, I've got something I need to tell you.'

'Yes, I know,' he smiled, looking up from his laptop. 'The interview – this time I'll play it your way. I'll be smart.'

That, of course, was not what I had to tell him. I paused for a second. This was going to take the wind right out of his sales. My next few words were going to change everything. Yes, I know, babies *do* change everything, but this could even change his interview. Actually, that's rubbish. It *would* change his interview.

'Yes.' I agreed. 'No more breezing in like a scruff bag.'

I decided to buy some time: 'I'll um, make another tea.'

'Cheers,' he said, with his face still in his laptop. 'Oh yes, and that bloke's leaving my flat too. Maybe we could move back.'

'That's great!' I said, adding, 'Assuming you get it.'

'I'll bloody get it,' he replied.

While the kettle boiled I did some thinking. You know, this could all work out fantastically well: Ben has a good interview and gets the job, I tell him I'm pregnant and we move into his lovely flat together. Happy days! In fact, happy *family* days. But there was an alternative scenario: I tell him I'm pregnant, Ben fluffs interview – or doesn't even do interview – no lovely flat and no money; unhappy family days. In fact, maybe no families at all.

I walked back with the two teas, put them on the table and sat next to him. 'Um, Ben.'

'Yup, Babe.'

'How long would it be before you heard?'

'About what, Lil?'

'The job – after the interview, I mean. How long before you know whether you've got it or not?'

'Oh, I'll get it,' he replied assuredly.

'Yes, I know, but…'

'Oh, maybe a couple of days,' he shrugged. 'I'll certainly know by the end of the week.'

'So a week from now?'

'Yeah, tops. Why do you ask?'

'Oh, nothing,' I replied. 'It'll wait.'

Ben

S hit and sugar. Life's ups and downs. First I get this call from the letting agents, telling me that the bloke who's renting my flat wants out – he can't afford to renew, apparently. So while they try to find someone else, I'd be back where I started – with a big mortgage and no income.

But under my new regime, the answer to bad news (or *any* news) wasn't going out and getting hammered, but staying positive. And the key to this, for me, was to go out for a jog. I'd found that jogging didn't just keep me fit – it helped me think positively too.

So within half an hour I had my trainers on and I was out there.

I'd been pushing myself further and further each week and by then was taking in a small park at the base of the hill called Ladywell Park. And as I ran, I got to thinking that perhaps this bloke vacating my flat was for the best. Maybe I could get someone in on a month-by-month basis. That way I could not only save the letting agent's fee, but go back in there as soon as I found a job.

The more I ran, the better this idea seemed. I imagined myself back there – going for jogs around Clissold Park and, in the same way that I'd been extending the run in south London, I could even, eventually, take in Finsbury Park and beyond – Hampstead Heath even!

I suppose the only negative thing about these thoughts was that, in hindsight, my imaginary plans weren't necessarily including Lily. It didn't occur to me at the time though.

The changes in me, at that early stage, must still have been subconscious.

Anyway, when I got back, guess what? There were two missed calls – both from the same number.

I returned the call and it was Nothing. Now, when I say was Nothing, I don't mean it was of no importance. Far from it. I mean it was this shit-hot new digital agency *called* Nothing.

It was a dead clever set-up. They had these really cool offices, broken into different areas. On the client side, where business matters were discussed, it was called Nothing Matters. Then there was the place where all the design work was done, and that was called Nothing Works. Oh yes, and the canteen was even called Sweet Nothing. And then there was the creative side, where ideas happened – and you guessed it: Nothing Happens! All a bit cheesy, I suppose, but right for the industry.

Looking at their web page, Nothing On, it's all white and minimalist and, well, sort of nothing-ish. But the main thing was – the thing that really mattered – was that they were absolutely *creaming* the crusty old agencies like my old place.

Anyway, one of there senior Creatives was leaving them and they needed a replacement. Could I come in for an interview? You bet I could!

So maybe jogging does work. Maybe it makes good things happen. Unlike getting hammered which makes bad things happen. Either way, it got me thinking. That first news – the flat becoming empty – wasn't so bad after all. If I could get this job, all those dreams, all those positive vibes that were running round my head as I was jogging, could yet come true.

When Lily came home she was delighted, of course. She told me that this time I should do it *her* way. You know, smarten myself up a bit, not be *too* confident, treat it more like a formal interview. Good council, I thought.

Even though I didn't actually have the job, I decided I deserved a little celebration – sorry, *we* deserved a little celebration. So I went out for a bottle of plonk and a takeaway Thai, but when I got back Lily was asleep on the sofa. She did wake up, but was so tired she made straight for the bed.

We'd been round to Mum's the night before, which was stressful for her, and then we'd had a bit of a row – which wasn't great – plus she had just done a day's work. So being shagged out was quite understandable.

I didn't have much else to do – I'd spent hours on the Internet and knew everything about Nothing, so to speak – so I switched on the TV, uncorked the bottle, opened the takeway cartons and worked my way through as much of the food as I could. Oh yes, and polished off the wine too.

I'd been watching some American made-for-TV rubbish but, because it was so full of absolute bollocks, I started to nod off. Anyway, it must have got to a commercial break because suddenly, up comes this music: *Blue-oo Loo, you saw me sitting alone.* I open my eyes.

Viewed sideways (I was still lying on the sofa) I saw the exact same commercial, for the exact same clients, that I was kicked out of my job for.

The fucking bastards! I got to my feet.

Well, as you can imagine, I was well pissed off. In fact, the more I came to, clearing my eyes as other commercials went by, the more pissed off I became. Livid, in fact.

The fucking two-faced, snakes-in-the-grass, fucking bastards!

I made straight for the phone – I was well up for it. After all, I'd had a few glasses of wine (a bottle, actually, plus some beers whilst waiting for the Thai). I got straight through.

'What the fuck's going on, Ned?'

'Hi mate, what's the problem?'

'Blue Loo's the fucking problem.'

'Look Ben,' he said. 'It wasn't my idea.'

'Too fucking right it. It was mine. You bastards!'

And with that I slammed the phone down.

That night, lying next to Lily, I couldn't sleep. The Blue Loo thing was going round and round my head. Then, after about half an hour, she stirred a little. You know, I'd actually forgotten she was there. She was lying next to me and I'd forgotten all about her. All that day – and now night – I'd been so wrapped up in my thoughts: *my* flat and *my* interview and *my* stupid Blue Loo.

Were my feelings towards her were changing? I started thinking about the whole Pherexosol issue. Was it just my imagination or was I changing back?

No, it was probably just my imagination. It had just been that kind of day.

Lily

Work, the following day, was awful. Firstly, I was late – something I very rarely am. Secondly, I had absolutely no lesson plan, or clue about what I'm supposed to be doing and, thirdly, I was feeling like crap.

I all but fell into the classroom, apologizing profusely and starting to rummage through my bag for books and papers and markers. To get them kicked off, the easiest solution is to write something on the board – something they can talk to their partner about. On the way in, I caught sight of myself of my reflection and my hair was a terrible mess; I suppose it was playing on my mind because, after I'd said a breathless good morning, I wrote up: *Have you had a haircut in the last week?* We were supposed to be doing the present perfect question form so it fitted, well, perfectly.

Almost before I'd finished, the little Korean boy, who sat in the corner, chimed up with: 'Why don't we say "*Did* you have a haircut in the last week", miss?'

I thought about this, but couldn't come up with an instant answer. I was exhausted, felt sick and my brain just wouldn't function. 'In some sentences we can say '*have you*' and in others we can say '*did you*', Ki,' I replied authoritatively.

'Yes,' he continues, 'but for this sentence, Miss. Is it: "*Did you* have a haircut in the last week", or "*Have you* had a haircut in the last week"?'

Then Maria, a clever clogs little Spanish girl chirped up with: 'Is it: "*Did you* have your lunch at two o'clock", or: "*Have you* had your lunch at two o'clock"?' This opened the floodgates with all and sundry chiming in with things like: '"*Did you* eat a McDonald's last night", or "*Have you* eaten a McDonald's last night"?'

By then I didn't give a shit about haircuts, lunch or McDonalds – or 'did you', 'have you' or pretty much anything. And then little Hanah, who's normally as quiet as a mouse, came up with: 'Have you had a good weekend… ?'

Without thinking, I cut her short and virtually screamed: 'No, I fucking haven't…didn't!'

Very quietly, with the rest of the class now shell-shocked, Hanah finished off her sentence: '… or is it, um, "*Did* you?'

Oh well, at least it bloody shut them up.

The afternoon lessons, if anything were an even bigger disaster. They were for a much lower level and, worse still, they were a communication class. The purpose of a communication class is to communicate. No grammar, no vocabulary, just talk. The problem is that the lower level students can't talk – in English, anyway. So to get them to do something – anything – you need loads of material, which means loads of preparation.

The activity I'd been handed required the most absurd amount of cutting up. Each student – and there were sixteen – had to have twenty little pictures of people doing different things – a girl playing tennis, a boy riding a bike, a man reading the newspaper et cetera – plus another twenty pieces of paper with these activities written on them: '*playing tennis*', '*riding a bike*', blah, blah, blah. By the time I'd finished – at a quarter-to-two and having had no lunch – I felt like Edward – or perhaps Edwina – Scissorhands. But then some idiot teacher opened the staff room window and they all blew up in the air like bloody confetti. So I just about had enough time to pick them all up again and sort them back into their piles before the bell went.

In total, the reading-up, photocopying and cutting-up time had taken precisely one hour, but the activity, once I got into the classroom, lasted under twenty minutes. Which left almost a whole afternoon of getting silent blood out of silent stones.

Anyway, on the way out, the Director of Studies caught me.

'Lily,' he said. 'I need to speak to you.'

He asked me into his office, offered me a chair and, rather ominously closed the door behind me. Once we were both seated, he cleared his throat, paused for a second, and then asked: 'Erm, Lily, is everything alright at the moment?'

'Er, yes, I think so.'

He looked down at a piece of paper in front of him before looking back up and saying: 'It's just that we've had a complaint.' He let the words sink in before adding: 'From one of the students.'

'One of the students?'

'Well, not actually the student, her parents.'

'Oh, I see.'

'There's no easy way to ask you this, Lily, but did you swear at her?'

'No,' I replied. 'Not *at* her, no.'

'But in the classroom?'

I nodded.

'Why was that, Lily?'

I hung my head. 'I was... well, flustered... and it just came out.' I looked back up at him: 'I've never done it before, I promise.'

'The problem is she's a Muslim, which makes it worse. Worse still, the agents she was booked through are our biggest clients.'

'I'm really, really sorry,' I said, very close to tears (at that point in my life I seemed to be permanently close to tears), adding a sobbed: 'What are you going to do?'

'Well, what *you're* going to do,' he said firmly, but kindly, whilst handing me a tissue, 'is apologize to the whole class tomorrow.'

Believe it or not, those words came as instant relief. At least it meant there was going to be a tomorrow – teaching-wise, anyway.

'And what *we* are going to do, as a school, is give you an official warning. We can't afford, under any circumstances, for this to ever happen again, Lily.'

Ben

It was Friday morning, the night after my rant at Ned. I was still semi-snoozing and only vaguely aware that Lily was running around the bedroom, throwing clothes, cursing and late for work.

In recent weeks, I had got into a habit of getting up early, going for a jog and making us tea in bed. But not that day.

I only awoke fully just after she'd left – to a room of strewn clothes, still-on light bulbs and echoing 'shit, shits' following her footsteps down the stairs.

I felt around for my mobile to ring her but couldn't put my hand on it. So I heaved myself up, rubbed my eyes and then my temples – then changed my mind and slumped back down again. An old, old feeling had returned.

To be fair, it wasn't a full-on old, old feeling; but it was still there. Dry mouth, throbbing head and regrets at things I might have said – or shouted. How shitty had I been to Ned? From memory, very.

My night's consumption – a bottle of wine and a few beers – was not enough for the real thing, of course. Not enough for the warring and the puking and the passing out. But it was enough to bring back those two old acquaintances – pain and regret. And, in a perverse, masochistic way, perhaps I'd missed them.

I made another effort at finding the phone – face down, arm out and rummaging. No luck. I felt my way down from the table to the floor, found it, brought it back to the bed, turned over, breathed deeply, cleared my eyes, found her number and hit it. Switched off. Oh well, it often is when she's at school.

I got up, made a coffee and came round a bit. I looked out of the window. The sun was up and shining and my head was already sorting itself out. I needed to un-burn a few bridges. I had definitely been over the top with Ned. He deserved an apology. After all, logically, it wouldn't have been him that ripped it off. For a start, after our combined piss up (I might be the one who was kicked out, but he got a bollocking too) he'd be unlikely to be back on that account. No, the culprit, almost certainly, was Tiny. He was the only Creative in the room.

I'd been a bit shitty with Ned about the whole Lily thing too. After all, we were longtime buddies from way before she came along. I could well imagine that he might have had his nose pushed out a bit and I should have been a bit more considerate. So I'd go up to town, buy him a drink and, hopefully, everything would be cool between us again.

But I had another reason for going to London. I thought I might give MediSee a visit too – they too had some explaining to do.

So I showered, shaved, dressed and said goodbye to an increasingly sceptical looking McFlurry (did he know something about me that I didn't even know myself?), then walked to Lewisham station and took the train to Waterloo East.

Once there, the walk to St Thomas's – it was a bright and breezy summer's day – blew any remnants of my headache away. Everywhere people were enjoying themselves – lying on the grass in Millennium Gardens, strolling along the South Bank, relaxing by the river.

Amazingly, Nurse Angela Harty remembered my name – greeting me with a cheerful 'Hello Ben, how are *you*?'

Imagine how many people had done trials since I'd been there, and yet she instantly knew my name? Now that really is a female thing. Despite a sober lifestyle *and* a quick bit of coaching from Lily, I still forgot names a second after being told them.

Having said that, I was able to reply: 'Fine Angela, and you?' (though her badge did rather help).

I couldn't remember the doctor's name though, so I just tentatively asked: 'I wonder if I could see anyone – you know, about the drug I tested here?'

I suppose it wasn't too common an occurrence, so after she'd kind of 'umm'd' and 'ah'ed' for a second, she replied: 'Er, I'll see if Dr Taylor is free,' (ah yes, *that* was his name). 'And what can I say it's about?'

'Oh, I just need some advice,' I answered, sounding as innocent as possible.

She disappeared for a minute, then came back smiling: 'Yes, he can see you now.'

She led me down familiar corridors, past unfamiliar inmates, and it all seemed so strange – going back and seeing different people going through all the things I'd been through. Sorry, *we'd* been through, I mustn't forget Lily. But if you've ever been back to an old school, or perhaps a place that you worked at for a long time, you'll know exactly what I mean. In some ways you're an imposter, but in other ways, *they're* the imposters.

She showed me into Dr Taylor's clean, bright office and he immediately stood up, shook my hand and, like Nurse Harty, asked how I was.

'Fine,' I said.

'So how can I help you?' he asked, sitting back down and gesturing to me to do likewise.

'Well, it's to do with this drug.' I settled into the chair and fished an empty bottle from my jacket pocket.

'Ah yes, Pherexosol.'

He then told me that he remembered me helping with the trials, said how well the drug had tested and asked me if I'd had any problems with it.

'Not problems as such,' I said, delving back into my pocket, 'but I did come across this.' I handed him a printout of one of the press releases.

To make the point clearer, I had highlighted the relevant parts: '*The majority of participants showed a greater predisposition toward romantic partnerships.*'

I gave him a few seconds to digest it then pushed another printout across his desk: '*This could encourage greater stability in romantic relationships.*'

I then handed him a third and a fourth – all saying roughly the same thing.

'Were you familiar with this?' I asked.

I could see him visibly blanching: 'Um, not at the time, no.'

'But you are now?'

'Yes.'

'When did you find out?'

'About halfway through the trials.' He coughed and slightly adjusted his tone: 'Look, you should really be addressing these questions to CalmerCeutical – they're the people who make it.'

'I don't know anyone at CalmerCeutical, Dr Taylor. And anyway, they didn't hire me – you did. I was dealing with you.'

He paused for a second then re-softened his voice. 'Look, Ben, it's not uncommon for a drug to have side effects. You signed a disclaimer…'

'I'm aware of that,' I interrupted.

There was a silence between us before he asked: 'Is this causing you some kind of problem?'

'Yes and no,' I replied.

'Go on,' he prompted.

I breathed in then answered: 'I don't know if I really love someone.'

He looked at me, looked back down at his papers then looked back up again.

'You're, er, not sure about your feelings?'

'I'm absolutely sure about my feelings,' I said. 'But am I, well, just a walking side effect?'

He smiled just slightly at this, then said: 'Yes, I can see how that could be, er… well, interesting.'

'Interesting! That's one way of putting it! Like I'm some kind of laboratory specimen.'

He breathed in deeply, sighed and said: 'Well, to some degree, that's exactly what you were. I hate to put it so bluntly, but that *is* the whole point of clinical trials.'

'But in this case, the specimen's my *whole* life – and Lily's. Our emotional lives, I mean. You're playing with people's very *being* here.'

'Oh, woah there, Mr Dryden,' he said, holding up his hands, '*I'm* not. Maybe someone at CalmerCeutical was, or is, but I'm just… well…'

'Carrying out orders?'

'That's not entirely fair. I was honestly unaware of all this before the trials started. In fact, to this day, I don't even know where they got all this information from.'

'You, I presume.'

'No, Mr Dryden, not the information about *Pherexosol*, the information about the *patients* – the statistics and things.' He picked up the page. 'All this "majority of participants" stuff.' He looked back up and said: 'I even saw one release that stated: "Seventy-five percent of those tested". Now how do they know all that?'

He handed me the printouts.

'This information didn't come from you?' I asked.

'No. How could it? We're not in contact with patients anymore – how would *we* know?' Then he paused before saying: 'I thought perhaps *they'd* contacted you. Mind you, that would've surprised me too.'

I was becoming more convinced. By him, at least. Maybe I was questioning the wrong man. Something else was going on here and I don't think it was of Dr Taylor's making.

I'd taken up enough of his time; I was running late now too, so we wound things up. We walked back down the corridors and, when we got to the reception, I thanked him – and Nurse Angela – and said my goodbyes.

The only problem was, I'd gone into MediSee with one question and come out with about six.

Lily

On the bus home, after my bollocking at the school, I found myself reflecting miserably on the whole bloody episode. For what it's worth, the grammar point that had kicked the whole thing off came down to just two words: '*in the*.' In English, we use the present perfect '*Have you had a haircut?*' because it's a generalization; but use past simple: '*Did you have a haircut last week?*' because the 'last week' makes it more specific. But because I'd added 'in the' to the sentence it's reverted back to less the specific, as in: '*Have you had a haircut in the last week?*'

Whatever. Who cares? The main point is, on such minor issues, major episodes are spawned. Rather like contraception (or lack of it) I suppose. Except that's not just about episodes, it's about babies: people. And that thought made look at things in a slightly different way. The enormity suddenly hit me. Whether or not I got a bloody grammar point right rather paled into insignificance.

Up until then, I'd been thinking about me, or perhaps me and Ben, or at most, me and Ben and a baby. But this wasn't a baby, it was *a person*. The responsibility, the decision – termination or otherwise – was huge. Easily the biggest decision anyone could ever make. Don't get me wrong, I wasn't about to go all pro life. It was still my body and it was still my life. And I certainly wasn't ruling termination out. It was just that replacing the word 'baby' with the word 'person' somehow brought it all home to me.

I looked out of the bus window, at the people making their way home. To them, it was Friday night and the start of two days off. To me, it didn't matter. When you're worried sick, there are no breaks.

As I walked from the bus stop, with the weight of the world on my shoulders, I realized just how much I needed to unburden myself. I was so, so looking forward to seeing Ben and telling him all about my shit day and my final warning. He would make everything all right, I just knew he would.

As I pushed the door open to the flat, I also decided that I had to tell him about the baby – the *person* – too. His bloody interview would just have to look after itself. My sanity was more important.

'Hi Ben,' I shouted, as cheerily as I could manage.

Nothing. The place was neat and tidy, unlike how I'd left it, but it was also empty. Oh well, I thought, he's probably out jogging.

My first port of call was the loo. With pregnancy comes endless piddles – or it did with me. The next thing – almost but not quite as urgent – was to trade my working clothes for my nice comfortable dressing gown. Every part of my body ached: neck, back, feet, except, perversely, my tummy. As I stripped, it was really noticeable that my nipples were larger and darker. To me, that is. To Ben, clearly not. It's amazing isn't it? Men spend their lives transfixed by the things, but don't even notice the obvious.

I shuffled back to the sofa, slumped down onto it and put my feet up. Relief!

I was tired, but sitting there, suddenly starving too. All week, I'd found myself getting instantly hungry. My sense of smell had rocketed and I could smell food almost anywhere. Ridiculously, at that moment, I could smell cheese-and-onion crisps. How that was possible, in an empty flat, was anyone's guess. I certainly wasn't going to argue with my body though, so after a couple of blissfully motionless minutes, I hauled myself up and went to the kitchen (I'd taken to buying those extra large packs).

In the centre of the worktop, before I'd even reached the cupboard, I saw it:

'*Hi Love. Gone to town, pick Ned's brains re Nothing. Won't be late, but you prob home first. Hope you had good day. C U later. Love Ben. XXX*'

Oh well. My unburdening would just have to wait. I opened the cupboard. Damn! Crisps would have to bloody wait too; the sod had eaten them all!

I found a few cheesy biscuits, the next saltiest thing available, went back to the sofa and munched at them. What I really fancied was a pizza – a regular Friday night treat for us. I suppose I could have phoned for one myself, but I assumed Ben would be back soon and that was one of his little jobs. Anyway, if there's one meal that's best shared, it's a takeaway pizza.

I closed my eyes thinking of yummy melted cheese, olives and stuff, and must have drifted off because when I awoke it was dark. I'd taken my watch off when I'd changed and the nearest clock was by the side of the bed. I stood up and stumbled over to the glowing green figures and squinted at them. 10:42? Can't be right. I leaned over to the cabinet and picked up my watch. Yup, quarter to eleven.

I sat down on the bed. He said he wouldn't be late. This is definitely late.

It was probably a product of my condition, but, like hunger, tiredness and a million-and-one other unwanted visitors, paranoia could rise almost instantly. Suddenly, all sorts of horrible scenarios flew up in front of me.

I scrabbled for my mobile, found it and rang his number. As it rang, I had this cold fear that it would be answered by some psychopathic mugger. But after a few rings, no mugger. In fact, no answer. But I did get the reassurance, albeit slight, of hearing his voice on his mailbox. I left a message and put the phone down – and did some more worrying.

I decided that worrying and waiting would get me nowhere. So I got up, put on my pyjamas, took off my make-up, cleaned my teeth, looked at myself in the mirror – now I looked worn out *and* worried – left the bathroom, got myself a drink of water and got into bed.

I'd taken as long as I could to do these things in the forlorn hope of a returned call. Which hadn't come. Okay, so fifteen minutes is a decent enough time to wait.

I tried again.

Ben's voice! Thank God!

But within seconds, my mood changed. There was this mayhem down the phone. No wonder he didn't hear me the first bloody time! His voice was slurred and he sounded as if he was in the middle of some kind of war zone.

A soppy 'Hi love' was followed by loads of background *shhhs*, *shhhs*, then giggles, as he (or she?) tried unsuccessfully to quiet things down. Then, after some ear-piercing female screaming, I just about caught: 'Woz jusht gonna ring ya.'

This was followed by more screaming, then laughing and shouting. Then there were more exaggerated *shhh*, *shhh*, *shhhs*, followed by: 'Gotshum great newsh', then more female screaming and general chaos.

Furious, I rang off, slammed my mobile on the bedside table and threw myself back down on the pillow.

Got some good news has he? Well so have I. Whether he thinks it's good or not, I couldn't say. But hear it, he bloody well will.

Ben

Having spoken to MediSee, the next task I'd set myself was the one I was dreading the most. I needed to apologize to Ned for being an arsehole. And in an ideal world, dependent on his reaction, I would then carry on up to town to buy him a couple of beers. Alternatively, he could tell me to sling my hook and it would be the end of a long-term friendship.

Now I don't know about you, but I've often found that the things you dread the most are the things that often turn out the best. And as I leaned on the Embankment wall, overlooking the Thames, that particular phone call turned out to be no exception.

'No, it was my fault,' he replied, almost before I could say sorry myself. 'I should've told you what Tiny was up to, but I didn't want to piss you off – I suppose I was hoping the whole idea would just go away.'

'Yeah, but I still shouldn't have lost it. It wasn't your fucking fault.'

'Nah. I would've done exactly the same thing – been well pissed off.'

So we both agreed to disagree on the whole fault thing, and when the conversation moved on and I asked if he was free for a beer, he went one step better.

'How about lunch?'

'Yeah, love to – where?'

'The Club, maybe?'

'Terrific.'

'One-ish?'

'Yup, great. See you then.'

Life just got better. Like the old days. Me, Ned, The Club and Friday.

It was a really beautiful day and I had some time to kill. So I decided to walk it. Crossing Hungerford Bridge, the Thames was grey green, the Houses of Parliament honey yellow and the sky bright blue. Leicester Square was full of punk-for-the-day tourists, in their union jack T shirts and candyfloss hair. Chinatown was all scarlet and gilt and hanging red ducks. And Old Compton Street was as vibrant as ever. Suddenly, dowdy old London was available in full HD.

On the corner of Compton and Dean, I bumped into a mate called Sam. He ran a small editing company and had originally helped me put together my showreel. We gossiped about the business for a few minutes, and then he said: 'Oh yeah, good news for you then!'

'What's that?' I asked.

'Nothing?' he said, with a knowing smile on his face.

'Ah, right, yes. You've heard.'

'Everyone has – good news travels fast.'

'It's only an interview.' I shrugged.

He gave me a rather sceptical look. 'Yeah, right.'

'Honest,' I protested.

He dragged on a fag and said: 'You do know the anti-smoking account's moving there, don't you?'

'*No!*' I said.

'Yup. They've pulled it from your old gaf.'

'And… given it to… Nothing?'

'Yup,' he repeated. 'And given it to Nothing.'

It took me a few seconds to take the enormity of this in. So *that* was the reason for the knowing smile.

You see, I'd always got on really well with this guy called Aaron. He was the main man at the Department of Health – looking after anti-smoking – and we'd worked on the award-winning stuff together. Now if Aaron had moved his account to Nothing and Nothing was now chasing me, the reason was obvious. Nothing was under starter's orders from Aaron – *their own client* – to hire me. The job was in the fucking bag!

I said my goodbyes, promised to catch up and continued on my almost singing, dancing way.

By the time I strode into The Club's dining room, I was more than just buoyant, I was on walking on air. I could see Ned, perfectly window-seated, overlooking the Prince Edward Theatre. But even before I got to him, weaving through the tables, I'd shaken hands and shared smiles with about half the diners. This little duck was very much back in his water.

'Hi,' said Ned, getting to his feet and greeting me like a long-lost buddy.

'Hi,' I replied, hugging him. 'Sorry,' I said, repeating my earlier apologies.

'Don't mention it, like I said, it's me that should be saying sorry.'

We sat down and he poured me a large glass of red.

'Have you heard?' he asked.

'About?' I replied, half-guessing.

'You *have* heard,' he smiled.

I'm not good at concealing things, especially from mates, and my face must have given it away.

He took a big swig: 'So we lose a major account, and you've got yourself a job.'

'Not necessarily,' I shrugged.

He went on to tell me that Tiny was raging about losing that account and that it was a serious blow to the agency. But losing it to Nothing, which was set up by an ex-employee, didn't help either.

'But the biggest embarrassment,' he explained, topping up his wine, 'the real kick in the gonads, would be if yours truly ended up working on it.' He looked at me thoughtfully before adding: 'I would imagine the board might have a few questions.'

'What goes around…,' I smiled, before going on to tell him, as I had to Sam, that it was only an interview, nothing more.

'Yeah, but that's just a game, isn't it.'

'Is it?'

'Yeah. They're hardly going to tell you it's a foregone conclusion, are they? It'll stop you being so... ' he paused before adding, 'demanding.'

'I see what you mean.'

'Yeah, just don't sell yourself cheap, that's all,' he said.

He then confided that, despite the fact that it was his lot losing the account, secretly he was well pleased – and would be double pleased if I got the job.

'But obviously don't tell anyone I said that,' he said. 'Next, it'll be me being kicked out.' Then he chuckled before adding 'Hey, wouldn't that be a laugh. *I* end up working for *you!*'

We both laughed at that scenario, whilst ordering another bottle of red and a couple of steaks.

As we neared the end of the meal, talking about everything and anything, I was already feeling it a bit. The heavy wine was fighting a battle with a medium steak – and the wine was winning.

Ned settled the bill, which was generous, but always going to be the case – he was on expenses, I was on benefits. He said: 'Your turn next.' I hoped he was right.

We repaired to the Dog and Duck – Soho's tiniest pub – where drinkers spilled onto the street on normal days, but simply took it over on warm Fridays.

As ever, it was crammed full of film people, most of whom I'd worked with. Loads of faces I knew. Amongst the guys – mostly editors and sound engineers – there were Sammy, Stevie, Ollie and the two Jamie's. And amongst the girls – mostly producers and schedulers – there were Lottie, Bellinda, Issy and Clare. Oh, and there were a sprinkling of advertising guys too.

On a warm day, red wine makes you drowsy, so cold lager is the answer. Pints of Stella, therefore, were next. It was all quite sane and civilized at that point; babbling away to each other in the sunshine – exchanging stories, laughing, hanging out. Just like the old days. But as the sun dropped, the tempo rose – and voices became louder, jokes became cruder and legs less steady.

A sudden image of Lily flashed through my mind – she'd be getting home soon. It was the first time that afternoon I'd even thought about her. How different to a few weeks ago, when she'd been on my mind every waking moment of the day.

I toyed with the idea of giving her a call, but decided it was just as easy to simply go home – I could still be there at roughly the same time she would. I could give her the good news in person. But before I knew it, another drink was put in my hand. Oh well, I could still be home *just* after her.

We were still all over the street, when the first cab turned up. I say 'first' because apparently there was going to be a posse of them, but I was all a bit oblivious to what was going on. You see, I'd vaguely been catching snippets of conversation about some party somewhere, but I hadn't really been taking it in. I wouldn't, would I? I was going home. Wasn't I?

Anyway, I got in the cab because I thought I was being dropped off at the nearest Tube. There again, by then, I could have been thinking total bollocks. After all, the nearest Tube was just round the corner – it would have been easier to walk. Or perhaps stagger. What I can tell you is that a few lines of charlie were going down in the back of that cab and I wasn't going to miss out. Well, it had been a while, hadn't it? Listen, I'm not making excuses. There *are* no excuses. I'm just telling you what happened.

Anyway, we – that's me, Ned and a couple of the girls – eventually all fell out of the cab, literally, at some big old house in what I now know to be Cricklewood. Frankly though, it might just as well have been the Lake District.

I vaguely remember us stopping off for some booze nearby and I also vaguely remember that the house was already rocking. There were people everywhere. Someone described it as a dinner party that had gone wrong. Well, it looked pretty right to me.

In no time, the night had flown by. It's an amazing thing; the more you drink, the faster the time goes. Have you ever been at a party and not drank? Don't fucking bother. The clocks virtually stop – usually at around ten-ish. Maybe that's the whole point of drinking: to shorten your life. Anyway, talking of time flying by, at some point I got a call from Lily. I honestly can't believe that I hadn't already called her. Surely I had? I know, that's it! I probably tried to call but I couldn't through!

There was this girl there. I can't even remember her name. Actually, I'm not even sure I even *knew* her name. Anyway, we danced for a bit (well, fell about and supported each other) and snogged (as much as two totally inebriated people are capable of directing their lips at each other) and there was a point where we definitely *could* have had sex (or she could have, but maybe I couldn't have). Either way, the point is we didn't. And I'd like to think that was because of Lily. My mind was too fuzzy to say that Lily was *definitely* the reason why, but that's what I'd like to think.

At some time that night, with the music still thumping somewhere, I must have fallen asleep. Where, I'm not entirely sure. A floor somewhere. I certainly remember a radiator digging into my back.

As far as I can recall, a whole twenty-four hours – and a Friday twenty-four hours at that – had gone by without me even calling Lily. Okay, she had made brief, incomprehensible contact with me, but that's not the same. I should have rung her. Worse still, apart from a few flashes here and there, I hadn't even *thought* about her.

What was happening to me? It was the medication. Had to be. The only time I'd ever been a decent bloke, in my whole life, was when I'd been on it. Now I was a cunt again.

Oh, don't get me wrong. I'm not using it as an excuse. If it were the other way around, then maybe yes. But remember, I was reverting to my *normal* self. I can't blame the drugs for that. Well, not the legal ones, anyway.

And getting even more deep and philosophical about it – is having no excuses somehow an excuse in itself? Does admitting I've been a cunt – like the Catholics do (well, sort of) – somehow make me *not* a cunt? No it doesn't. If having no excuses is an excuse, then the original excuses wouldn't be an excuse. And I'd simply be a cunt all over again. Which I was.

I woke up, or sort of woke up, at some time the next morning – feeling like cold, shivering shit. There were a few other people around, picking their way between beer cans and vomit – all hushed and grey – like ghostly undead.

I didn't get far, because when I stood up – or half stood up – I felt worse and had to collapse again – this time on a sofa. Some time later, through the French windows, like some surreal apparition, Ned appeared. I've got no idea where he'd been. I don't think he did either. We didn't say hello or anything. We were like silent strangers, with some terrible, shared knowledge.

A few moments later I crawled to the toilet and vomited… viciously.

Just twenty-four hours earlier, rather stupidly, I'd said I'd missed that old, old feeling? Acid vomit and guilt.

Well, Ben, this was it. In full-on, head thumping, Dolby Sensuround. And it was just about the worst feeling in the world. I deserved it, of course. That's why God does it. Acid vomit, guilt and pain. As for Lily, she was just drifting away.

I think I dozed off again, but anyway, when I awoke, it was probably early afternoon. My returning friend, as I became conscious again, was nausea. I just about made it to the toilet, where I puked again, before slumping to the base of the toilet, in a time-honoured pose. Some time later I got up and made it to a sink, where I drank loads of water – despite it making me feel sick again.

When I awoke for the third time – or was it the fourth – some clearing up had been done. Then Ned turned up again. He said we should go. Just those three words: 'We should go' – whispered almost – and we went.

We wandered to the nearest station, the sunlight slightly morbid and sepia, like us. The station turned out to be Cricklewood (Ah yes, that's how I know!). We waited on the bench for ages. When the train trundled in, as slow and somber as our mood, there were people all dressed up for West End shows and stuff. It made my transgression seem even worse. The whole world had moved on. Except me.

When we got out of the train, we dawdled to Ned's, where I drank more water, he boiled a kettle and we both sat in silence. I decided it was time. I needed to ring Lily.

I'd worked out this fiction. Drunks are good at that. I'd apologize and grovel, of course. But I'd also tell her the party was at Ned's and, as I was only around the corner from my old flat, that's where I'd slept. You know, to check it out, because it was empty again.

Then, I could mention us moving back in there together. You know offer some hope, some brightness to offset the shit – maybe that would help.

So I rang, but got voicemail. Well, I expected it, really. She picks up mobile, my name comes up, she doesn't answer. What would you do?

So I apologized and apologized to a recorded message, said how stupid I'd been and told her the little fiction about the flat – and said that I'd make it all up to her somehow. Oh yes, and I gave her the option of me staying away that night too. You see, I had no choice but to go back to her place because of my interview was Monday. But if she didn't want me in her flat that night – which I could fully understand – I'd stay at Ned's for what remained of the Saturday. Considerate, aren't I?

Lily

Saturday was awful. My standard shoulder to cry on, Suzie, was away. I did consider ringing my sister, Jen, but I didn't really trust her anymore. That's an awful thing to admit, but it's true. She'd let me down badly over the whole lab trials thing, so who's to say it wouldn't happen again? Anyway, big sisterly advice was something I could do without. I even considered going to home for the weekend. Obviously I wouldn't have told Mum and Dad anything, but the familiarity and the comfort – and the company – would have been nice. But I was probably in the wrong frame of mind. My nerves were so shredded, I probably would've ended up rowing with Mum – again. And anyway, it needed a train journey and a pick-up from Dad and a journey back. I just couldn't face all that.

So I spent Saturday aimlessly walking and thinking and sometimes, when no one was looking, crying. Yes crying. My life was now an utter mess.

Only a short while ago, before Ben had come along, everything had been simple. My job was going well, I was saving up for another trip, and of course, I wasn't pregnant. Four months on, my savings were gone, my job was on the line and my boyfriend – sorry, ex-boyfriend – was absent, both physically and mentally. But all that would have been just about okay, if I hadn't been pregnant. Carrying a baby – *a person.*

Is there any decision that anyone, anywhere could take, as important as this? Politicians, businessmen, clerics – do their decisions match the one I had to make? Do men even *comprehend* that?

With no one else to ask, I spent half of Saturday and most of Sunday on Ben's laptop (he might as well have some use) looking up the FAQ's about terminations on websites – NHS, the Brook and Marie Stopes, et cetera. These were some of the words and phrases that seemed to come up time and time again:

'*Non-judgmental advice*' (like I cared about other people's fucking judgment! It was my own judgment – and guilt – that scared me).

'*Easiest under 12 weeks*' (I was probably about 9, but it still didn't sound exactly easy).

'*Free on NHS but must be referred through GP*' (Fair enough).

'*Private Treatment Also Available – Easy Payment Scheme*' (Easy and Payment: oxymoron).

And here are the choices:

Abortion pill. Womb contracts and sheds lining. Embryo lost through vagina. Can be painful. Can cause vomiting. Can cause diarrhea.

Surgical termination. Tube put in uterus. Suction applied. Neck of womb stretched. Forceps remove foetus.

Medical / surgical termination. Heart of the foetus is stopped.

And so the last thing I needed as I was working through that lot was a soppy, apologetic, puppy-dog phone call from Ben.

It was about five o'clock on Saturday afternoon and McFlurry, my final friend, had persuaded me to retire to the sofa for some serious kneading – something he hadn't been getting much of since Ben had pitched up.

When my mobile rang, breaking the silence – McFlurry's purring apart – it triggered a little pang in me. You know, I knew who it was. Despite the lack of contact for almost twenty-four hours, I somehow knew it was Ben. And, if I'm truthful, I hoped it was too. You see, although things hadn't been so good over the previous couple of weeks *and* despite the fact that he'd been out all night, one little part of me – or perhaps big part of me – still loved him.

But I didn't answer it. I could have disturbed McFlurry and checked out the caller, but I didn't. God, McFlurry had been disrupted quite enough over the past few months. I owed him that, at least. Eventually, it stopped.

Sure enough, when I finally got up to make a tea, I checked the missed calls and the last one was from Ben.

I made my tea, sat back on the sofa and, as McFlurry prepared to re-mount, played it back.

What bollocks it all was; full of groveling apologies and lame excuses. Amongst other things, he generously offered to stay away for another night. Generously – try cowardly! Having said that, it probably wasn't a bad idea. I probably would have knifed him – or worse still, forgiven him and told him about the baby. And that really would've been a mistake. Why? Because I needed to make cold, clear, unemotional decisions. You see, I was certain that, like all soppy blokes, he would be over the moon – oozing promises of never-ending devotion and fatherhood. And he'd mean it too. But what blokes say and what they actually *do* – long term – can be entirely different. A week earlier, I had been on the verge of telling him. By Friday, if I'm completely truthful, I was less sure. I mean, we'd both been tetchy with each other. And yes, on balance, telling him still seemed like the right decision. Since Friday though, and his all-night piss-up (and who knows what else) I was less and less sure.

So it wasn't so much that I couldn't afford to give *him* the option – I knew what his reaction would be – it was that I couldn't afford to give *me* the option - of believing him.

After I'd listened to his message, I spent some time thinking and perhaps my stance softened a little. Maybe I was being a little harsh on him. It was a Friday and he was celebrating a new job. Well, sort of. Oh yes, and on the voicemail, he'd mentioned something about his flat. His beautiful, wonderful, spacious, two bedroomed (one for the baby) flat. Simply heaven. Me with a baby, him with a huge salary and us in a beautiful home. Colour magazines come true. So maybe, just maybe, I would tell him.

He'd get a bollocking first though.

Ben

The Saturday that started on a floor in Cricklewood ended on a sofa at Ned's. Why the fuck do I do it? I can't think of another drug, or another anything, that gives you as bad a return as alcohol. Think about it. From Friday afternoon onwards, I'd spent about ten hours drinking and generally feeling good. Then there were perhaps another three or four hours, in the middle of Friday night, when I can't say I felt anything – mainly because I can't *remember* anything. From then on – from first thing on Saturday, to well into Sunday, I felt like crap. So for every hour spent feeling better than good, I got back two hours feeling much worse than shit. What kind of return is that? There again, I *was* out of practice, I suppose.

Ned, however, wasn't. And by Saturday night he was up for it again, asking me if I fancied joining him for a 'quiet' night playing pool with some of the lads down at the local. No, I didn't. So I stayed in, sat on the sofa and just thought.

Perhaps, after all, I wasn't like the old me. But if I wasn't like the old me, I wasn't exactly like the new me either. The new me would never have gone out on the lash leaving Lily at home in the first place. And the new me certainly wouldn't have seriously considered copping off with a girl I'd never met either before. So what was I? Maybe just the brief product of some medication that was now slowly wearing off. So did I really love Lily? I honestly couldn't say.

Then I thought about the conversation I'd had with Dr Taylor. I'd kind of accused them of putting chemicals into people that made them fancy other people. Manipulating people's emotions.

So what did alcohol do, then? Why had I fancied that girl at the party? True love? Hardly. So it's just the same, isn't it?

Fed up with endless agonizing over it all, I sat in Ned's flat and flipped through some of his magazines.

In one of them, *Nuts* I think, I saw this quote. It was from some C-list celeb – recently kicked out of some jungle – and he'd come up with this wonderful insight into maleness: '*Blokes are capable of divorcing the sex from the person. If they see a great pair of tits, they see a great pair of tits. They are independent. Not actually attached to anyone.*' When asked if it was the man who is independent or the great pair of tits, he answered: '*Both.*'

Profound. Truly, a giant amongst men.

Is that the life I wanted? Unattached tits? Frankly, I no longer knew.

Before Lily (and Pheroxosol?), life had been straightforward. Now, absolutely nothing was.

When Ned finally came back from the pub, he brought with him Brendan and Gary, a couple of mutual mates from another agency. Unsurprisingly, all three of them were well and truly plastered. But despite the drink, and the huge, carefully crafted spliff (for them, not me) their mood remained muted – compared to a Friday or a Saturday, anyway.

I'd never really thought about it before, but looking at it as an outsider, from a sober perspective, it clearly wasn't only *how* you partied, it was *when* you partied. No matter how much you consume – if it's not a Friday, it's not a Friday. So instead of being high spirited and happy, they were morose and maudlin.

This was best illustrated by a conversation all four of us had whilst sitting around the bottle-littered table, just before Brendan and Gary finally called it a night.

We'd been talking about me getting back into the business, with them all backslapping, telling me that the world of advertising just hadn't been the same without me and how wonderful I was, in a sloshed, over-sentimental way. But of course there is a flip side of all that slushy stuff, and after a short silence Brendan tiredly announced: 'You know, we're all fucked.'

'Whatcha mean?' slurred Gary.

'Fucked and shallow, ev'ry one of us,' he replied throwing his arms out limply. 'Everyone in advertising, I mean.'

'Fucked and shallow?' asked Ned.

'Yup, fucked and shallow,' confirmed Brendan.

'Yeah, I agree,' concurred Gary, warming to his theory, 'We're *all* fucked and shallow, ev'ry one of us,' before adding: 'And you know what?'

'What?' replied both Brendan and Ned – in slurred unison.

'The only way to *not* be fucked and shallow is to *know* you're fucked and shallow – that's how I shurvive.'

Being the only sober one there, this needed some clarification: 'Let me get this straight,' I asked. 'Everyone in advertising's fucked and shallow, and the only way to *not* be fucked and shallow is *to know* you're fucked and shallow?'

'You got it,' confirmed Gary.

'Yeah,' agreed Brendan and Ned.

In not grasping this theory, I was clearly in a minority of one. Of course, the lack of drink and drugs could have been a factor.

'But I'm not fucked and shallow,' I replied, a little defensively.

There was a long silence whilst Brendan thought about this. Then came his reply: 'Then you're fucked and shallow.'

And deep down, he may well have been right.

Lily

He came back on Sunday at about eleven – smelly, unshaven and apologetic.

I'd just sat down on the sofa and had the cat on my lap when I heard the key scrabbling in the latch.

Knowing it was him, I looked towards the door and I saw him a fraction of a second before he saw me.

You know, when you see someone first, you sometimes get a chance to judge their feelings – their true feelings – before any kind of mask goes up. And I would say that at that infinitesimally brief moment in time, his true feelings were relief, mixed with remorse, mixed with – just possibly – love. That or he was a bloody good actor.

'Well,' I said, stroking McFlurry. 'The prodigal returns.'

'I'm sorry,' he said, casting his eyes downward.

'And so you bloody should be.'

He didn't reply to that. I suppose he had the sense to realize that no response was probably his best response.

'These are for you,' he said, lifting up the bunch of bright red glads he'd been holding limply by his side. 'I thought they'd cheer the place up a bit.'

'Sure needs it,' I said, getting immediately up and walking away from him and towards the kitchen (dislodging a glaring McFlurry in the process). 'Oh yes,' I added, 'and the place needs clearing up too.' I pointed towards the Hoover I'd only just grappled from the cupboard. 'I was just about to start the housework.'

'Can't we talk?' he sighed.

'About what?'

'Well, for a start, I'd like to say I'm sorry.'

'Okay, you've said it – a number of times, if you include those stupid messages.'

He sat on the chair, his jacket still on, his hand to his forehead: 'Look, I'll do the hoovering later, but we need to talk.'

'About what?' I asked for the second time.

'Well, everything, I suppose,' he answered.

And everything, sort of, is what we did talk about. Not absolutely everything because I didn't *quite* bring up the subject of my pregnancy. And that was because some of the 'everything's' he mentioned rather worried me. You see, amongst other things, he came up with: 'You see, I've been a bit fed up lately.' This was delivered head bowed, not looking me in the eye.

This fed-up-ness, apparently, was because of his lack of work, lack of money and the living together in such a cramped flat. I say 'apparently' because I don't think it was that at all. There was something else.

Let's take them one-by-one. The work thing he should have been over the moon about – he certainly had been on Friday night! And that also solved the lack of money thing. Which only left the 'living together in a cramped flat' thing. The 'cramped flat' issue looked like being sorted when his flat became vacant. Which just left the 'living together'.

So it seemed to me that the living together was his real 'everything' issue – not spoken, but inferred. Which brings me to another 'everything' – in this case, *my* 'everything' issue. Was the reverse true? Was I also getting fed up with living with him? Of course, I had every right to be after that weekend. But even without that, was I cooling off too? At exactly the time, in my condition, that I shouldn't have been?

Of course, because none of this was actually said, we both made all the right noises – about all the other 'everything's.' He placated me about my work problems and I told him he'd do well at the interview.

That afternoon, somberly, he cleared the flat up and I went out for a walk. Alone. Thinking again.

And later on, in bed that night, both awake, but looking up into the dark, he said the actual words: 'I'm not sure anymore, Lily.'

I didn't need to ask him what he wasn't sure about. I knew exactly. Because I wasn't either.

What a fucking mess.

Ben

The night before the interview, in our bed, in the dark, I cried. Not because of the interview, of course, but because of Lily. So that was another first for me. Big, tough Ben. Crying over a girl. Or perhaps it was out of frustration. You see, it was over. She knew it and I knew it.

Earlier that afternoon we'd been discussing our problems and it seemed to me they were about more than just work and money and stuff. And the other thing was, even though it was me that brought the subject up and even though it was me that had fucked up the weekend – or perhaps *because* it was me that fucked up the weekend – she seemed to be thinking the same things.

I suppose I had a sort of excuse, if you could call it that. I'd stopped taking that fucking stuff. Of course, I didn't tell her that. Why would I? She seemed to be feeling the same and as far as I knew, she *was* taking it. Anyway, it would have sounded ridiculous – and what's the point of carrying on a relationship that relies on chemicals?

And so later that night, lying in the dark, I said: 'I'm not sure anymore, Lily.'

I knew she was still awake but she didn't say anything. She just turned over. She knew what I meant.

And I actually cried – well, shed a tear. Like I said, it was out of frustration, probably. She didn't hear me though. At least, I don't think she did.

The next morning when I awoke, she was up already, sitting on the sofa.

She was just sitting there, looking at nothing. I put my arm around her and told her that I did still want to see her. I wasn't calling it a day or anything – if she wasn't – I was just admitting the way it was.

We talked for a while, with perhaps me talking more than Lily. We didn't row or anything. Neither of us actually said it was over. We didn't say I'd be moving out either, but it was understood. We just decided to leave it at that. For now. I'd come back after the interview, see how we both felt, and sort it out. You know, like grown ups.

There was one other thing though. It was strange, as if there was something she wanted to say, but wouldn't. There again, perhaps I was just imagining it.

Lily

I slept little, just tossing and turning and thinking. I got up, put my dressing gown on, made a tea and sat on the sofa – while all the time, he snored. Amazing, isn't it, how blokes can just sleep. Then again, after the weekend he'd had, I suppose it wasn't surprising.

As I sat there, the first bird sang, then two, then a chorus. The dark became grey, then pallid, then white. And all the while the curtains softly moved.

I was looking away from him, but he eventually woke at six, or maybe seven. He came over, sat next to me and put his arm around me. I don't know why.

He said nothing, so after a long silence I said: 'So that's it,' whilst still looking straight ahead. It was both a question and statement.

'I do still want to see you,' he replied, quietly.

How ridiculous. He does still want to see me. Should I tell him? That simply seeing me wouldn't be enough? I'd need more than just seeing. *We'd* need more. There were three involved.

What would the point be, though? He either wanted me or he didn't. And I certainly didn't want him to want me because I was pregnant. How long would that last? And anyway – and here's the crunch – did I want him anymore?

While I'd been sitting there and he'd been sleeping I'd had loads of time to think. And some of the things he said the day before had made no sense. So after a while, after he'd made us a tea and sat back down again, I asked him: 'So what was that phone call all about – on Saturday. You know, about your flat?'

He didn't answer, but he knew the call I meant: the simpering, apologetic one.

'You talked about us living there. You said if you get the job we could move in.'

'And I meant it,' he replied, almost at a whisper.

'Sorry Ben,' I said, raising my voice slightly. 'Last night you said you weren't sure. Now you're saying we could move into your flat. I'm confused.'

He thought for a second and then replied: 'Yes, and so am I – that's the problem, I suppose – that's why I said I wasn't sure.' He then sighed deeply: 'Maybe I just need more time.'

What I'd like to have told him, was that time's the one thing he *didn't* have. Nor me. Two weeks, tops – to make the biggest decision of my life. But again, if I'd told him that, I knew the answer I'd get. And I wanted real answers. Based on love and commitment, not duty – or soppy, here-today-gone-tomorrow promises.

So I didn't take it further, we just left it at that, quietly. He needed to go off for his interview. I needed some sleep. Monday or not, I certainly wasn't going to work.

Mercifully, I slept well – waking up at about eleven. And, just as mercifully, when I awoke Ben had gone. I really couldn't be going through all that again.

I had already decided what I'd do with what was left of the day; if possible I'd meet up with Suzie. You see, what I needed more than anything was a friend. I was hoping she'd be free for lunch, so I rang her, and fortunately she was. Actually, she probably wasn't. But as soon as I rang her, she said yes. Suzie really *was* a good friend at that time.

I got McFlurry some late breakfast – while he wound circles round my legs – got dressed, and walked to the bus stop.

It's only a short bus ride from Lewisham to Bromley but it's plenty long enough to think. And the more I thought about the situation the more I had the feeling there was something else. Something left unsaid. It was as if Ben was on the verge of saying something, then not quite saying it. There was definitely something missing.

Then something dawned on me. The whole thing had been pretty sudden. Okay, possibly he'd been keeping it hidden a while, but I don't think he was that good an actor. So I thought: when a relationship goes pear-shaped, what's often behind it? Someone else, that's what. So was there someone else?

I had absolutely no evidence, but it did make me wonder. Again, like a million other things, it was something I'd mention to Suzie – see what she thought.

Bromley is like a thousand other towns. Pedestrianized, uniform and dull. Not just the shops, the people. Don't get me wrong, I wasn't putting myself above them – far from it – I was pretty dull and pedestrianized too. But sitting outside Costa Coffee, waiting for Suzie, I was struck by the mundaneness of it all. Mind you, it was that kind of weather too: grey, nondescript, oppressive.

At about ten past one, along came Suzie, hurrying, smiling and brightening my life. She gave me a big kiss, we both ordered toasted cheese sandwiches and coffees and got down to talking – we had lots to cover. You know, I honestly don't know how blokes survive without true friends. When I say true friends, I mean people you can tell your troubles to. As I understand it, all they do is get drunk and talk bollocks. How does that help anything?

Anyway, Suzie did manage to clarify things a little. Basically, she pointed out that I only had one really big decision to make. Baby yes, or baby no. The Ben issue was obviously intertwined, but it really wasn't the main one. If it was baby yes, I simply had to tell him. But if it was baby no, then I could tell him – it was his mess too – but I didn't have to. I could just finish with him. Either way, the main decision was still the same: baby yes, or baby no.

The next point was the timescale of that decision. That was simple. I had perhaps three or four days, no more, to decide. If that decision *was* termination it would need to happen a about week after that. And termination or not, I still needed to see my GP and therefore I needed an appointment by the end of the week. Suzie was tough on me on this one, instructing me to 'just get it done *now*, Lily'.

So I picked up my phone, hit the surgery number and sat there, half-listening to Suzie and half-listening to a recorded message moving me slowly up the queue – eventually getting a appointment for eleven o' clock that Friday, just four days time. Oh yes, and Suzie, bless her, said she'd come along with me.

You'd think that with all the worry and the thinking and stuff, I wouldn't have been hungry. But pregnancy doesn't seem to work like that. By the time I'd finished my toasted sandwich – including every single crumb and all the little dollops of cold, melted cheese stuck to my plate – I could have started all over again. But it was almost two and Suzie was due back at work, so I didn't.

I hugged her, thanked her profusely and said I'd see her on Friday – but that I'd be ringing her before then anyway – then made my way to the bus stop.

It was on the way home that something dawned on me – hit me like a thunderbolt, in fact. It all harked back to a conversation I'd had with Suzie earlier. I'd told her about Ben's apparent sudden change of heart – and that maybe there was another woman involved. She'd said she doubted it, but that if there was, he was obviously a complete tosser. Either way I shouldn't agonize about it for the moment. 'I know it's difficult,' she'd said. 'But try to put that out of your head for now – you've got a far bigger decision to make.'

But going home on the bus I found it almost impossible to divorce the two issues. You see, it might not sound very feminist but, like it or not, you can't separate an issue like whether someone loves you or not from the decision to have their baby. Even the issue as to whether he does or doesn't get a job is tied up too. And even, more practically still, whether we can or can't move back into his flat. And that was the thought that hit me. That was the thunderbolt. His flat!

There was this big, big hole in his story concerning his claim to have stayed in his flat on Friday night. How the hell did he get in? If he took the keys with him, it would have been because he was planning a visit – so he would have told me beforehand – which he didn't. Even if he was only going to put his head round the door he would have been absolutely bubbling about it. And if he *didn't* take his keys, he couldn't possibly have got in. After all, estate agents aren't famous for being open at midnight, are they? And there was yet another problem with his story. When he'd originally told me about his flat becoming vacant, I was pretty sure he'd said '*in a couple of weeks*' – and that was only a week ago.

As soon as I got home I made directly for the kitchen drawer. I rummaged through it, and soon found them – exactly where they'd normally be – pushed to the back of the drawer, behind some string, a box of matches and some batteries. Okay, he could have put them back before going off to the interview, but wouldn't they then be at the front of the drawer with all the other keys?

I slammed the drawer closed, left the kitchen, found the sofa, sat down and thought deeply, almost rigidly.

There was one very simple way to find out. It was certainly sneaky, but I think it was justified. I picked up my mobile and made a call.

'Ah yes, hello there. I was wondering if you had any flats to let in the Church Street area of Stoke Newington?'

'Yes madam, quite a few.'

'Well, ideally it would be two bedrooms – you know, a Victorian conversion with a garden. Park Street would be absolutely perfect.'

'Er, let me see. Yes, in fact we have a perfect match. Park Street, two bedrooms, with garden.'

'Is that the park end or the Church Street end?'

'Erm, let's see. The park end I think. Yes, number 17.'

'Brilliant. Could I view it this afternoon?'

'Well hopefully, but I need permission from the occupant first – can get back to you?'

'The occupant?'

'Oh yes, it's still occupied, but only for a week. He leaves next weekend.'

Now I know it's rude to just put the phone down on someone. But that's exactly what I did. Stunned.

Ben

L ily was sleeping while I got ready for the interview but I still took her advice. We may not have been on the best of terms but that didn't make her wrong on what to wear. I had one very expensive suit – a navy blue Ted Baker – and I wore that, together with my Hugo Boss shirt, but without a tie. All very sharp, but just on the casual side of cool.

I looked in the mirror. Yup, I looked the part. It was just a pity that, deep inside, I didn't feel it. The whole interview thing, given the situation with Lily, had turned into something I could have done without.

You might find this a strange analogy, but I've always thought suits are kind of like Marmite jars. Even if you're empty inside, you remain uniformly full on the outside. In fact, I reckon there's an advertising campaign in there somewhere. Anyway, I'm sure it did the trick for me, masking my inner emptiness and making me look confident. To the man in the street I probably strode down the road assuredly, stood on platforms stylishly and rose up escalators effortlessly. Inside though, there was nothing. Then again, I suppose that was pretty apt, because that's exactly where I was going: Nothing.

Their offices were in Clerkenwell, and though it's supposed to be the new Soho – über cool bars and media types – it also has a whiff of the City about it. So you do see more suits around than in the West End. So yet again, Lily's advice seemed okay.

When I got there, Nothing had no number, nor a sign, nor a logo. In fact, it had Nothing – just big blank windows.

Inside was just a huge space – white as a fridge – eight, regimentally spaced, transparent chairs and a clear, apparently self-levitating reception desk. Above this desk (also in white and therefore almost unreadable) was John Cage's profound sentiment: *I've Got Nothing To Say And I'm Saying It.* Below these weighty words, seated at the desk, was a girl with angularly cut blonde hair, high cheek-bones, a sharp white trouser suits and an expressionless face.

Suddenly, I was really pleased I'd ponced myself up. This lot meant business.

I walked up to her and introduced myself. She just about flickered an expression, asked me to take a seat and said nothing more – I didn't even hear her tell anyone that I was there. She must have done her job though, because as soon as I'd perched myself on the edge of one of the Perspex chairs – and even though I was a full fifteen minutes early – I was greeted by this guy in a suit, called Simpson.

Simpson the suit. Worked at my previous place. Not a great friend – a bit oily for my liking – but it was good to see a familiar face at such a time. In fact, as he led me from the reception, making slightly strained small talk (well, strained for me, anyway), it was pretty obvious why they'd let him loose on me. You see, I knew how these things worked. They had assigned him to show me round because we already knew each other, because they were hoping he would make me feel a bit more at home. And that's not really a strategy you'd use for any normal interviewee, is it? Therefore, this wasn't going to be any normal interview. Everything really did point towards me getting this job.

He took me through white corridors, into silent spaces and even out into a peaceful, almost Zen-like courtyard. And in all that time, I only saw a handful of people. At one stage we walked into a large blank room – empty, apart from a chair, a desk and a laptop – and he said to me – in all seriousness – 'The reason it's empty is we fill these spaces with ideas.' He then went on to rather smugly explain their strategy: 'You see, we believe in minimum. We feel most companies have over-cluttered their images – and we remove that clutter.'

The more I saw of the place, the more it spooked me. No, worse than that, scared the shit out of me. It seemed to be a mixture ad agency, design shop and business consultancy. "Dystopian" is another of those poncey words I'd never normally use, but it fitted this fucking place - Brave New Hell. But was it me? I couldn't imagine this lot partying on Fridays.

As we walked around near-empty spaces, Simpson was beginning to really piss me off:

'All our clients,' he said, 'are top-end, blue-chip; most of them are online, as are our ads, so we're comfortable with this *so-called* recession stuff – it's just High Streets who've got it wrong.' He then paused, laughed and added: 'Half of them need bulldozing anyway; just tat bought by losers.'

So that made this very genuine recession '*so called*', our eked-out weekly shop '*tat*' and Lily and I '*losers*'. Nice. He continued in this vein around the rest of office – telling me about 'bankrupt business thinking' – until we found ourselves back at the reception, where Paul, my old colleague, was waiting.

Paul had changed since we worked together too. Okay, he always wore a suit, but back then it was sort of crumpled and lived-in; now it was even sharper than mine – plus a silk tie, plus a floppy hanky. And talking of floppy, I couldn't remember his hair being quite like that either.

He shook my hand vigorously, said I looked well – which I didn't exactly feel – and led me towards his office.

It was after that, as he pushed open his office door, that my mobile rang. I suppose, in hindsight, I should have just switched it off – but I hit the green button. You don't always think that quickly in stressful situations, do you?

All I could hear was screaming – plus a few words like 'fucking bastard' and 'bloody liar' and 'cheat', something about me spending the night with 'some fucking whore' – oh yes, and that all my clothes were now in the front garden.

BBC Television Centre

Paul Fletcher sat in his cluttered little corner, surrounded by the tools of his trade – his BBC computer, his own personal laptop, three telephones (internal, external and mobile) and piles of newspapers, magazines and periodicals.

He picked up his external phone and dialed. Eventually the phone was answered by a chirpy-voiced girl: 'Good morning, CalmerCeutical, how may I help you?' He asked to speak to William Wyles, their CEO, and was put on hold until another woman came on the phone. She asked him pretty much the same question and also put him on hold. Finally a man's voice came up: 'Hello, Wyles here, how can I help you?'

'Ah yes, good morning. My name's Paul Fletcher, I'm a researcher for Breakfast TV, and we're thinking of doing a piece on one of your drugs.'

'Er right, yes,' replied Wyles, cautiously.

'And we were wondering if you give us a bit of background on it?'

'Erm, possibly. But it depends what it's about,' replied Wyles, even more guardedly.

'Well, we came across a little piece in the *New Scientist* on Pherexosol and…'

'… Ah yes, Pherexosol, that *is* one of ours.'

'Yes, well, according to this article it could have hidden benefits – you know, apart from making people happy and stuff.'

'Possibly,' replied Wyles, almost, but not quite correcting him on his rather unscientific terminology. 'What have you read about it?'

'Well, it said it might help with relationships – like a sort of, well, a love drug.'

Wyles gave a rather sniffy cough. 'It rather depends what you call a *love drug* Mr… er, sorry, I missed the name.'

'Fletcher, Paul Fletcher.'

'Yes, well if you're thinking along the lines of an aphrodisiac, I'm afraid you're way off the mark.'

'No, no, from what we understand it could *stabilize* relationships – and maybe even get them started in the first place – you see, we thought it could make a really interesting human interest story.'

Suddenly, lights flashed in Wyles' brain. This could be *exactly* the break he was looking for.

'Well yes, I imagine it would. Which programme did you say you're working for?'

'Breakfast TV.'

Jesus! Millions of punters!

'So, er, what do you want from me?'

'Well, I thought you could give us some background – from the horse's mouth, so to speak.'

'I'll do my best, but I may have to refer you to our CSO – if it gets too technical, I mean.'

It didn't get too technical. Far from it. Fletcher was asking all the right questions – when, where, how – you just couldn't *buy* publicity this good.

Fletcher then asked: 'The articles – they mention that some of the participants are now, well, couples, yes?'

'They certainly are – or were, up to a few weeks ago.'

'Have you kept in touch with any of them?'

'Not as such, but we do keep records, obviously,' replied Wyles.

'You see,' said Fletcher, 'The thing is, this type of story works so much better if we can get the actual people into the studio.'

'Actual people?'

'Yes, one of the couples. Can you imagine how good a story that would be?'

'Um, yes,' replied Wyles, trying to remain businesslike and not overdo the enthusiasm bit. 'I suppose that's what human interest *is*.'

'Indeed. We just need to find the right couple.'

Lily

I was absolutely beside myself. Enraged, apoplectic, incandescent. I completely lost it – screaming and shouting down the phone, telling him to fuck off in as many ways as can be squeezed into about fifteen volcanic seconds.

Now let me just say this: I'm not a violent person. I'm a teacher. I vote Liberal. I even read *The Guardian* when I can afford it. Therefore, I believe in rationality and in working things out peacefully together. But I just couldn't help myself.

I started throwing his stuff about. Not in any particular direction or order, just throwing them about, sometimes twice, mostly randomly. Then *not* randomly: out of the window. Clothes, shoes, digital camera, CDs, shaving stuff, his stupid Millwall shirt – the lot. Then, having run out of things to throw, I rather illogically picked up my own mobile phone – the bringer of bad news – and tossed that out too. I don't know why I did that. It was stupid. And I can't say throwing his stuff out made me feel an awful lot better either. I know it's supposed to, but it honestly doesn't.

When I'd finished I collapsed on the bed, face down, and sobbed and sobbed. Not exactly the action of fighting feminist, I grant you. But in my defense, my hormones were all over the place.

After about an hour I got up and went to the bathroom. My tired, smeared face looked back at me from the mirror. I really needed to get a grip. So I washed my face and then decided I needed some air. I pulled on a cardigan – it was a typically grey

London day – opened the door, stepped over Ben's belongings and went downstairs.

Fortunately, I found my mobile phone easily. It was in the middle of the flowerbed. Or weed bed. I put it in my pocket and walked. Nowhere in particular – just walked.

Lewisham, if anything, is worse than Bromley. Mind you, with the view I had of the world, anywhere and everywhere was crap. It was school holidays so there were lots of kids about. I don't know whether other women could confirm this, but you do notice babies and young children more when you're pregnant. Sadly, what I saw didn't exactly inspire me.

One of the things that really struck me was that the children, generally, were dressed up like adults, and the adults, generally, were dressed like children. Little girls with tarty earrings, mums in crop tops and dads in ridiculous shorts and baseball caps – almost like schoolboys. The same men who probably spent their entire schooldays trying to *not* wear shorts and peaked caps. There again, who was I to disapprove? At least they *had* families. Some of them were even of the two-parent variety. Just because my life was a mess didn't mean I had to be bitter and twisted about everyone else's.

I continued to wander, away from the High Street and down a side road, until I came to a small urban river, the Ravenbourne, I think, running through a high-rise housing estate. It wasn't exactly beautiful, but it did at least have water in it – albeit running between concreted sides. There were benches there. Some of them even had unbroken rungs. So I sat down on one and meditated upon the river. After a while I noticed movement near the water's edge. Surprisingly, there were little pondy things swimming around in it. Amazing! Even there, hemmed in by concrete, against all the odds, was thriving, wiggling life.

After a few more minutes I pulled out my mobile. I kind of knew what I'd find. Two missed calls. Oh well, let's hear what the stupid sod has to say.

'*Lily, look, I know you're pissed off with me, but it wasn't like that. You're right I didn't stay at my flat. I stayed at Ned's. Telling you that was stupid and I'm really, really sorry. I was just trying to… well, to make it all seem better, I suppose. But I honestly don't know what you're talking about. There is no other woman. Please ring me back.'*

Great! He admits he lied – outright, bare-faced – *after* I find him out. Now he tells me there's no other woman – *after* I find him out. Erm, let me think now… Oh yes, I'll just believe him. He's bound to be telling the truth!

I could have chucked my bloody phone in the river. But I didn't. Sitting there in the brightening weather – the sun had suddenly come out – I had a feeling of tranquility, inevitability.

I put my phone back up to my ear and listened to the second message.

'Hi Lil. You didn't return my call, and I don't blame you. I hoped you would, but I didn't expect it. There's something I really should have told you. I've been thinking about it for ages. It's to do with you and me and the drug trials and everything. It's really important. I can't tell you on the phone because it would just sound stupid. I'm coming home to pick my things up – I honestly don't care about them being in the garden or whatever. That's not important. You are. I really need to see you – if it's possible. But I won't make a big deal if you don't answer – it's your flat, your life, not mine – I'll just go. But you could call me back if you get a chance.'

I sat and thought, then played it back again. *'There's something I really should have told you. I've been thinking about it for ages.'* Yes Ben. There's something *I* really should have told *you* too. I've been thinking about *that* for ages too.

'It's to do with you and me and the drug trials and everything. It's really important.' What was all that about? What on earth did drug trials have to do with anything? They were months ago!

Ben

Interviews are supposed to be two-way things aren't they?
This one wasn't.

I sat there, white-faced and shell-shocked, not really
taking in a word he was saying. I suppose I did murmur
something occasionally. I vaguely remember him asking me
what I'd been up to lately, and me absent-mindedly replying:
'Er, nothing much.' After a brief pause he asked how long I'd
been doing this, nothing much, to which I answered: 'Oh, ages.'
Not ideal, I would imagine.

After a while, with him running out of things to say and me
glancing at my watch, he asked me if I had any thoughts about
compensation. I just asked him what he meant.

'You know, *money*,' he replied.

'Oh that,' I shrugged. 'Dunno.'

After I'd returned a few more silences and noncommittal
grunts, he'd clearly had enough. So he breathed deeply, looked
up at the clock and said something like 'I imagine you've got
things to do.' I took the hint gratefully, got up and made straight
for the door. Then I realized I hadn't even shaken his hand. So
I stopped, went back, said a brief goodbye and made straight
back for the exit. Thinking about it, it probably wasn't the best
interview I'd ever given.

Hurrying along the street, I grappled for my phone, scrolled
down to Lily and hit connect. I don't suppose I looked any
different to thousands other thirty-somethings – hurrying past,
smart suit, smartphone – but never has the Marmite analogy
been nearer the mark. On the outside: dog's bollocks; on

the inside: alone and empty. And as her phone just diverted to voicemail for the umpteenth time, I found myself feeling lonelier and emptier. You just didn't know what you had until you lost it, did you, Ben? Smartphone, dumb-arse.

I took the tube back to London Bridge and when I emerged into bright sunshine – the weather had been as changeable as my moods – I called her again, and again got voicemail.

This time I told her, or nearly told her, about the whole Pheroxosol thing. The only reason I didn't actually mention the name, or go through the whole story, was because I thought it would sound ridiculous on a message. But now, more than ever, I was certain Pheroxosol was the factor.

After all, I'd only stopped taking it for just over a week. In that time my whole life had crashed. Hadn't exercised once, back on the piss, done coke in a cab and could even have shagged an unknown woman on an unknown floor. But most of all, I was on the verge of losing the best thing – sorry, the *only* thing – I'd ever had.

When the train got to Lewisham, I all but ran to Lily's and, slowing to her front door – past bits of discarded clothing – I rummaged for my bunch of keys but couldn't find them. Ah yes, I remember. They were spoiling the lines of my oh-so-cool suit. So I punched the bell. And waited. Nothing. I rang it again. Waited again. Nothing again.

I pressed the intercom: 'If you're in there, Lily,' I called, 'there's something I need to tell you.' Again, nothing.

Just then, Jimmy, the guy from downstairs, turned up. 'Hi mate,' I said. 'Can't find my keys.'

'No worries,' he said, talking through his cigarette.

He threw away his fag, pushed through the door and I followed him – thanking him as I went. He turned right into his flat, I thanked him again and continued ahead up the stairs.

As I neared the top I passed more clothing: underpants, socks, a shoe, then another shoe. When I got to the landing it was like a fucking Primark sale. Stuff piled everywhere. I stepped over it and hammered the door. Nothing. I hammered again – and waited again. Still nothing.

I hung around for perhaps ten minutes and reluctantly decided to go. Perhaps she'd gone to Suzie's, or maybe her parents. Either way, it was pointless hanging around. Perhaps Ned could put me up.

Then I heard the door open downstairs. Then footsteps. Lily's footsteps.

Lily

The minute I walked through the front door I knew he was there. I don't know how, but I did. And as I walked up the stairs, passed the clothes I thrown, into my vision came his 'interview' shoes, then his posh trousers, then his face. We looked at each other. At first he said nothing, but then he said: 'I'm going to go if that's what you want. I haven't come to cause any trouble or anything, so don't worry.'

I was almost at the top of the stairs, blocking his way out. He walked towards me, but it was towards the exit too, so I assumed that's where he was going. I moved to let him past – hardly possible on those stairs – but he stopped short. The distance between us was probably less than it had been for days.

'You still need to know the truth,' he said.

I could have given him the obvious answer. I could have said yes, that I still did need to know the truth, but the truth kept bloody changing. Or I could have asked which version he was referring to. But I didn't. Didn't say anything – just looked at him. All the other parts of his face could lie to me, but not his eyes. If he *was* going to tell me the truth, that was where to look.

'There is no other woman. Never has been. Believe me Lily, it's the truth.'

He then moved a step closer. 'You see, I now know what's been going on – with me, I mean – and that's why I should probably go.' Then, given what he'd just said, he said something astounding. 'I love you Lily.'

Just to make it even more ridiculous, he then added: 'But the reason I love you is the problem.'

He loves me, but he has to go? Because of the *reason* he loves me? What rubbish!

'Sorry Ben, you've lost me.'

'The medication,' he answered.

'What medication?'

'Pheroxosol. It's what's keeping us together – or *was*.'

I just stood there looking at him, with all his stuff in his arms. I couldn't understand a word he was talking about.

'Look Lily, this isn't a trick or anything, but could we just go inside – to talk, I mean?'

I looked at him. Even though he was talking utter crap, for some reason, I decided to hear him out. I walked past him, opened the door and let him in behind me. I didn't want it to be an open invitation to hang around, so I avoided the sofa – way too intimate – and made for the kitchen. I leaned my back against the table and looked at him.

'Go on then,' I said.

'You know that Pheroxosol,' he said.

'Of course.'

'Well, it has this side effect. Don't laugh Lily, because it sounds ridiculous, but it makes you fall in love.'

'*What*?'

'It makes you fall in love.' He then edged a step closer. 'Think about it, Lily. Think of all the people at the clinic. How many paired up?'

I found myself thinking about Francine and Johnny, and Russell and Sophie, and Josh and Claudia. He was right, maybe. *Maybe.*

'You see,' he said, 'I found out on the Internet. It's all to do with dopamine and oxytocin and stuff.'

I couldn't believe I was hearing this. Generally, he was such a cynical sod. He just wasn't into conspiracies and stuff. Complete bollocks, was how he described all that.

'I know what you're thinking Lily,' he said, pretty much reading my mind. 'But this isn't people's blogs and stuff. This is *New Scientist… The Financial Times.*'

'But come on Ben, makes you fall in love? *Makes you fall in love* – you can't *make* people fall in love.'

'Maybe you're right. I don't know; you could be. But it seems a hell of a coincidence. You see, I found all this out about two weeks ago, so I stopped taking them just to see what would happen and… well… since then…'

Then it hit me. Like a thunderbolt. Two weeks ago was *exactly* when I stopped taking it too.

I hadn't intended sitting down with him; making him feel at home, but I was absolutely thunderstruck. I just pulled up a chair, almost in a daze, and sat down.

He pulled up a chair opposite me:'Be truthful Lily, what did you think of me? You know, the first time we met – before the drug kicked in?'

My mind rapidly returned to the idiot that had turned up at the clinic, the oaf who was lying on the floor outside my room. If he were the last man in the world…

'Come on Lily,' he repeated 'What did you think of me?'

'I thought,' I said, very quietly, 'you were a dickhead.'

'Precisely, I was. But that's not the point. The point *is*, you weren't even vaguely interested.'

'So you're saying that the only reason we… well, liked each other…'

'Loved each other, Lily.'

'Okay, but you're saying it was just, well, because of stuff we were putting into our bodies?'

'I don't know Lily, I just don't know. But at the very least you can see why I'm confused, can't you? And you can see why the idea of a long term commitment scared the shit out of me *and* why I stopped taking it – to see.'

After thinking for a second I looked at him and just said:'Ben.'

'Yes,' he answered.

This was the moment. There was no point in leaving it: 'I haven't been taking it either, since… well, for roughly the same time.'

I left it a second, almost willing him to ask me the reason why. Then he did:

'Why?'

'Because I'm pregnant, Ben.'

Ben

S he was pregnant! Amazing! Fantastic! Ten or eleven weeks, apparently. She told me about it when we were talking about the Pheroxosol stuff. Oh yes, and on that very subject, she'd stopped taking them too – exactly *because* she was pregnant. And *that's* why she'd also been so moody of late. Actually, you can take your pick on that one – she could have been moody because of the lack of it, or because of *my* lack of it – or simply because she was pregnant. All three probably.

We were sitting together at the kitchen table when she told me. I went straight to her, hugged her and told her it was the most wonderful thing I'd ever heard. She said she expected me to say that – which I suppose wasn't the answer I hoped for. She clearly wasn't as delighted as I was. So I asked why. She said that the problem was that when a girl gets pregnant to a bloke like me they *always* say that sort of stuff.

I felt inclined to ask her how many times she'd been pregnant to blokes like me, but I didn't, of course.

'Well what would you *like* me to say?' I asked, pulling back a little. 'That I was disappointed?'

'It's not what you *say* that matters, Ben. It's what you *do*.'

'Well, what should I do then?'

'You could start by being a little more realistic,' she said, gesturing at the room. 'I mean, look where we're living for God's sake.'

'Well,' I shrugged, brightly, 'I might get that job.' Then I remembered the disastrous interview.

'Why didn't you tell me this earlier, Lil?'

'Have a guess,' she said, fixing me a look. 'Would you have liked me to tell you when you were at that party? Or perhaps when you were at Ned's – *allegedly*. You know, I don't think you even *begin* to understand.'

She then looked down at her fingers: 'You know, Ben, when I was a kid I had this teacher – Mrs. Campbell. And she once asked me what I wanted to do when I grew up. I told her I wanted to meet a nice man and have a baby – to look after. She laughed at that, of course. But the point is, I'd always assumed that it was a two-stage process. You know: man, baby to look after – two different people.'

She did have a point. But it wasn't the kind of point that that I had much of an answer for. So I looked down at my hands too: 'So what are you going to do?' I said, half-knowing the answer she'd give.

'Well, up until a few minutes ago, my mind was pretty well made up.'

'You weren't going to keep it.'

'Correct,' she confirmed, bluntly.

I said nothing, perhaps hoping she'd say something further, but she didn't.

'So why are you thinking differently now?' I asked.

'I don't know that I am,' she said.

I didn't reply to that, but then she said: 'In lots of ways there are even fewer reasons to have it, aren't there – if the Pheroxosol thing is true. I mean, think about it – what's the point of bringing up a family based on that? What sort of future for a kid? Family held together by chemicals.'

'Yes,' I reasoned. 'But we're getting on okay now, aren't we? We could make it work. And anyway, that stuff could be… well, a sort of back-up plan – for when things go wrong.'

'Back-up plan? Come on, Ben. Anyway, *when* things went wrong, you mean.'

'Everyone argues sometimes. At least we'd know how to solve it. We'd have a choice. If we weren't getting on, we'd either try to ride out the storm or…'

'Or what? Are you seriously suggesting we base a baby's future – *our* baby's future – on a bloody nasal spray?

'Well,' I shrugged. 'Valium's not so different, people take that to get them through.'

'Well I don't. I want to love someone because I *love* them, not because of some fucking pharmacist.'

'Okay, but what about booze? How many relationships owe something, maybe just a little bit, to drink?'

'Not those that last.'

I'm not sure I agreed with her on that. Most people first meet up at parties and pubs, then they build up relationships in restaurants and stuff – all with the help of drink. How many of them would have even got off the ground? But I didn't say this, of course. I could see it turning into a row, so I just waved the white flag, said nothing and suggested tea. So while I boiled a kettle, dunked the tea bags and added the milk, she sat in silence.

I decided not to take them back to the kitchen table, but walked past her and put them on the coffee table instead. I then cleared all my rubbish off the sofa and suggested she came over. After a pause, she did. Better still, as she walked over, she asked me how the interview had gone. I don't mean better still because my interview was crap. I mean better still because it broke the ice a little, moved things on. So I told her how terrible it was but not to worry. There'd be others.

After that conversation had run its course, I said: 'Look, one way or another, we'll sort this all out.' I touched her hair. 'We'll get through it, I promise,' I said, and kissed her on the cheek.

'Was that you?' she asked, smiling weakly. 'Or the Pheroxosol?'

It was the first time I'd seen her smile in over a week.

Lily

That night we slept together. It probably wasn't a very good idea. You see, one of the problems with blokes is that they seem to think that sex makes everything okay again. To men, sex with an ex (and that, effectively, is how I felt) is like an MOT certificate for a broken down car. Rubber-stamp the certificate, switch on the relationship ignition – and you're back on life's road again – despite fundamental problems under the bonnet.

The other problem with hopping back in the sack, rather obviously, was that he was still there the next day. And indeed, the day after that (and yes, we had sex that night too). Which took me right up to decision day.

So there I was, doing exactly what I said I *wouldn't* do – on the verge of making a decision about the baby with Ben confusing my mind. Not that he was pressuring me or anything. It's that merely by *being there*, he was influencing my decision. That wouldn't have been a problem, of course, if I knew he'd *always* be there – and that was the thing I couldn't be certain of.

I went back to work over those two days – mainly to get away from him. It was the lesser of two evils. You see, I didn't want to be endlessly going over the same old ground with him.

But on the Wednesday afternoon, when I came back from work, things somehow started to click again. It was nothing I could really put my finger on. He did, and said, all the normal things – made me a tea, asked about work. But somehow, everything seemed natural again.

Maybe it was just tiredness – kind of giving in. Maybe it was just desperation on my part – wanting to *believe* it was alright again. Or maybe it was because he was on the Pheroxosol again – I'm not sure I agreed with it, but he meant well.

Whatever it was, that night, the night before I was supposed to go to the doctor's, we went to bed, *didn't* have sex and fell asleep in each other's arms.

I awoke the next morning having had a wonderful night's sleep for the first time in ages; for all kinds of reasons, pregnancy seems to play havoc with your sleep, so I was thankful for a full, blissful, eight hours. A luxury – miracle, even.

Ben was sitting on the bed next to me. 'Morning, Lil,' he said, holding the tea. I cleared my eyes a little. 'Morning,' I replied.

He then got back into bed and we snuggled up. It was good just being together.

I had never told him how imminent my decision needed to be. Being a bloke, it didn't seem to cross his mind. But I had taken the precaution of telling the school that I wouldn't be in that day. Now that day had come. I'd pretty much made up my mind. I wasn't going to have an abortion. Of course, I still needed to go to the doctor's though.

Ben asked me if I wanted him to go with me and I said no. I suppose there was still a one percent chance I might, just, change my mind back, and for that reason I didn't want him there. Anyway, I'm quite capable of going to the doctor's myself.

'In that case,' he said, 'I'm going to the doctor's too.'

'Really?' I asked.

'Yes, Dr Taylor – at MediSee – they've got some explaining to do.'

'I thought you said you've already done that?'

'I have, but things have changed.'

I wasn't sure I could really see the point of causing trouble, but I let him have his say.

'There are a couple of things I want to talk to them about. Firstly, there's the situation with you. I mean, don't get me wrong, I'm not blaming them for you being pregnant or anything.'

'I should think not!' I cut in. 'As far as I recall it was a certain part of your anatomy' – I kneed his groin – 'that saw to that!'

'Well yes, but joking apart, they need to be aware of what they're getting people into.'

'Perhaps they should have a health warning,' I said. 'Warning, this stuff makes you fall in love and have babies.' It was good that we could both joke about things a little more.

'Anyway,' said Ben, 'I want to get some more – in case we need it.'

'In case *you* need it,' I corrected.

'You know, Lil, I've been looking into this stuff, and some of the ingredients they've put into it are also produced naturally by pregnant women, stuff that makes them less likely to… well, how can I put this… more settled I suppose.'

'*Settled*! Oh, right. So you're saying the only reason I'm not off shagging everything in trousers is because of some chemicals *naturally* pumping round my body – whereas you, being a bloke, need a little medical help in that respect.'

'I didn't say anything about shagging,'

'Okay, let's say it's the reason I'm not as *anti-you* as I was, then – assuming I'm not, of course – but you might need a booster in that respect, to not be *anti-me*.'

'All I'm just saying is what I read – about pregnant women, I mean. Effectively, it said her body is telling her she's found her mate – so she doesn't need to attract another one.'

'Just don't count on it, cowboy.'

Okay, so I *was* playing along with all this, being kind of jokey. But he was treading on very thin ice indeed.

'Well, whether I'm your mate or not,' he said, 'with the signals your body's sending out, the last thing you need is more Pheroxosol – well, according to what I've read, anyway.'

'Whereas you do?' I challenged. 'To love me, you need a nasal spray?'

'No,' he rather over-hastily replied, 'What I mean is… well, maybe not now, but you're pregnant and who knows what could happen to us in the future?'

He was beginning to sound ever more defensive, so I kind of left it at that. I really didn't want to turn a joke into an argument. And anyway, I could kind of see his point. Kind of. If I *was* going to have the baby, anything that could keep us together was worth considering. After all, there'd be a child's future at stake too.

So I changed my mind about my agenda that day. As I wasn't having a termination, I could see my GP anytime – and decided to go with Ben to MediSee. You see, I was becoming as interested in the whole Pheroxosol thing as he was – I suppose I needed to be, didn't I. And anyway, a nice little trip down memory lane together would be just (if you'll excuse the awful pun) what the doctor ordered.

BBC Breakfast TV

As soon as researcher Paul Fletcher told his producer of the piece he'd unearthed, she loved it. And within half an hour of contacting William Wyles he'd received an email from CalmerCeutical listing the names, addresses and personal details – including photos – of the dozen or so romantically paired trialists.

These details had been passed to the director who quickly decided which couple to go for – the most glamorous looking, of course – and a production assistant was dispatched to make contact with them.

Because time was of the essence, the production assistant got straight to the point – informing the shell-shocked girl on the end of the line that it was the BBC phoning her, and could she and her boyfriend appear on live TV the following morning.

'Er, yes,' came the faltering reply. 'I'd er... I mean we'd love to... but...'

'Great! I'll tell the producer. She'll ring you within the hour.'

'But what it's about... I mean, why are we... ?'

'Oh yes, sorry, should've said – it's to do with the drugs you've been taking.'

'Drugs!'

'Yes, Pheroxosol – it's just been discovered that it makes you fall in love.'

'It makes you *what*?'

'Fall in love – You see, that's the reason you and your boyfriend are together.'

'The reason we're together?'

'Yes, look, I haven't got time to explain now. Is it a yes or a no? We do have other options, you know.'

'Well, I suppose it's yes… but…'

'Great, like I said, we'll be back within the hour – we can explain it all then.'

That's the way it works in TV. No time for pussyfooting about. No time for worrying about turning someone's whole life upside down in one phone call – telling them that perhaps their partner doesn't *really* love them. How can the media get away with it? Because, in the society in which we live, being a celebrity is everything. So no one says 'no' to TV, because there's always a chance it'll lead to something *really* important like an appearance on *Big Brother* or photos in *Hello*. And that's what people want, even more than love – ironically.

So in the middle of the following night the couple, dazed, confused and sleep-deprived, were picked up by cab and whizzed up the motorway to Manchester. They were then signed in, issued identity passes and led by a production assistant to a canteen where their passes allowed them a free croissant and a coffee. There they sat, nervously picking at their pastries whilst hoping to spot a passing celeb or two – which they didn't.

Twenty minutes later the production assistant returned and escorted them to the production office where a girl called Gemma, the producer, and a man called Stephen, the director, briefed them.

Amongst the information they were given were the questions the TV presenter would probably (though not definitely) ask them: Was it love at first sight? Was it *only* down to the drugs? Would they keep taking it? What of their futures?

Being breakfast news, the piece would be jointly presented by a male and female combination (male: camera left, female: camera right), but, as ever, their tasks would be divided. And because this particular piece was half scientific (well, sort of) and half love story (well, sort of), the director had decided that the male anchorman would introduce the medical, scientific stuff and his co-presenter the softer, fluffier stuff – i.e. the interview about their relationship.

That being the case, the anchorman would introduce the piece using some faux-scientific graphics illustrating how the chemicals work. These graphics had already been knocked up the night before, and consisted of a Photoshopped boy and girl with wobbly lines animating from his brain to hers – and vice versa, of course.

Once this introduction was complete the camera would then pan across the sofa to his co-presenter and her two interviewees. Only after all the questions were finished would the director cut back to the wide. This would show (from camera left) the male presenter, the female presenter, the male partner and the female partner. Of course, such technical details weren't passed on to the loved-up couple – all they needed to know was where to sit and when to open their mouths. The girl did nervously ask the director whether she would be allowed to hold hands with her boyfriend, though – to which the director, of course, said *absolutely*. In fact, so delighted was he with this idea (it added, as he put it, an *aaah* factor) that he'd later claim it as his own.

Nothing was left to chance, of course. A quick visit to hair and make-up made sure their skin tones were suitably dabbed down and their wardrobes were passable.

With the clock counting down (they had cut away to the local news) the couple were led in and plonked on the famous sofa.

All was ready – camera crew, lighting crew, production crew – and the director, looking at his monitor, was delighted with what he saw. What a coup beating the tabloids to it! No doubt they'd dub them the 'love-drug couple' or something. Whatever – the main thing was they looked great. Johnny, with his in horn-rimmed glasses and high cheekbones, was pure Hollywood. And Francine, with her sleek body and long chestnut hair, pure Paris.

Yup, perfect choice.

Ben & Lily

They strolled to the station hand-in-hand and when they got there, stood side-by-side on an empty platform. The weather was grey and the train was late. A typically English scene.

When the train did turn up, the doors slid open and he let her on first. They found a window seat together and snuggled into it, but said nothing. As they picked up speed, they watched South London silently slide by – railway arches, old factories grimy terraces – and he put his hand in hers. Just two ordinary people, one ordinary couple.

When they got out at Waterloo East they re-linked and walked hand-in-hand towards St. Thomas's. They didn't say much, but when Lily, out of the blue, said: 'I wonder what the others are up to now?', he knew exactly what she meant. And that's the way it works with couples. When it *does* work, that is.

'Yeah,' replied Ben. 'We should all try to meet up sometime.'

As they wandered along the South Bank, Lily noticed the pub where she'd had that disastrous, goatee-bearded date, just six months earlier. So much in six months.

When they got to MediSee, it was Lily who went in first, greeting Nurse Angela before introducing Ben – whom, of course, she already knew. This was because it was Lily who'd made the original appointment, and *this* was because Ben had feared that Dr Taylor might have been 'permanently unavailable' if he'd tried to fix it up himself.

So when Angela Harty stuck her head round Dr Taylor's office door and told him that both Lily *and* Ben were here to meet him, the doctor's heart sank just a little. Too late, there was nothing he could do about it.

He greeted them with handshakes, offers of tea (which they declined) and said how good it was to see them both (which it wasn't) before Ben cut the small talk with his bombshell:

'You see, what we'd really like, Dr Taylor, is a guaranteed lifetime's supply.'

The doctor was so stunned he laughed out loud. Yes, ex-trialists *can* continue with the medication but *for life*? Unheard of. And way beyond his remit.

'Look, Mr Dryden, you really should be talking to CalmerCeutical about this sort of thing.'

Ben thought about this: 'Okay, perhaps you should ring them, then?'

The doctor shuffled some papers, waffled something about being a busy man and basically, understandably, refused.

So Ben simply dropped the second bombshell: 'Um, Dr Taylor.'

'Yes, Mr Dryden.'

'Lily's pregnant.'

After a brief silence, whilst Dr Taylor collected his thoughts, perhaps struggling to comprehend the relevance of this remark, he replied:

'Oh erm, that's, er, nice, um… congratulations.'

'Well thank you. But the point is, we – that's Lily and me – might need Pheroxosol, to, er, to stay together. For life, I mean.'

'I see,' replied Dr Taylor thoughtfully, before adding: 'But I'm not sure that's our, erm, responsibility.'

'Well, yes,' replied Ben, 'Of course. We don't hold the drugs directly responsible. I'm, er, pleased to say that's Lily's condition is entirely down to me.'

Dr Taylor smiled at this: 'Good, so apart from congratulating you on your joyous news, I'm not sure how else we can help you.'

'Well the point is, even though we don't hold you *directly* responsible, we do feel you are culpable – and we were wondering about our legal position.'

'Your legal position is not my problem, Mr Dryden. You'd need to see a lawyer for that. Anyway,' he said, preparing to rise from his seat, 'as I made clear to you before, you signed a disclaimer.'

'Yes, but I'm not sure that would cover such an occurrence. I mean, that would mean we were tied into spending huge amounts of money – a lifetime's supply of an expensive drug – or suffer the loss of our relationship and perhaps even our family. And there's another point. You see I'd still like to know how the drug company, um, what were they called… ?'

'CalmerCeutical.'

'Yes, CalmerCeutical. I'd like to know how they obtained all the information about us. You know, what with data protection and stuff.'

'I don't think that's an issue here,' replied Dr. Taylor. 'You see, once the trials are complete, and they're what we call 'un-blinded', the drug company is perfectly entitled to have your details.'

'Ah, I see,' said Ben. 'So you *did* give them our addresses and stuff, did you?'

This was a rhetorical question. Ben knew perfectly well they hadn't – because Dr Taylor had told him so at their previous meeting. But he didn't wait for an answer. He simply pushed his point further: 'And then there's the question of the other details.'

'What other details?'

'You know, all that stuff in the press releases – about how many of us were seeing each other, about our relationships – *four months* after the trials were completed. Putting stuff in the paper about who's seeing who. How do you know that hasn't been compromising? Invasion of privacy, Dr Taylor.'

'As I said before, I've no idea where that information came from.'

He then shuffled his papers again, indicating that the meeting really *had* come to an end. 'As I've said before, I really do think you should be addressing these questions to CalmerCeutical.'

'And as *I* said before, I don't know anyone at CalmerCeutical. And anyway, we were dealing directly with you – not CalmerCeutical. MediSee was on the paperwork we signed and MediSee paid us. Whether you like it or not, your company is responsible.'

'So what do you want me to do? I doubt we've even got *a month's* supply of the bloody stuff.'

'Well like I said before, I want you to call CalmerCeutical – if that's what it takes.'

'*Now,* you mean?'

'Yes *now*, I mean – or we take it up with the Medical Council.'

Dr Taylor very nearly told them to do just that. He was pretty sure MediSee were in the clear. Then again, was he? That point he'd made about the paperwork was a good one. Maybe he should just pass all this over to CalmerCeutical – wash his hands of the whole damned thing. It was their ruddy cock up, after all!

So rather reluctantly, Dr Taylor picked up the phone, pressed the speed dial, exhaled wearily and, when it was answered, asked for William Wyles. When he finally got through he exchanged a few pleasantries and then said:

'You're, er, not going to believe this William, but there's a couple of the Pherexosol trialists here in my office and, um, well, they're after a rather large quantity your drug.'

Wyles then asked him how large, and Dr Taylor coughed nervously before replying: 'Enough to last them, er, ha-ha – their lifetime.'

Wyles laughed at this too, so Dr Taylor quickly went on to tell him about Lily's pregnancy, but leaving out the bit about Ben's legal threat. He felt sure he would need to bring that up eventually but for now he rather forlornly hoped it wouldn't be necessary – why stir up the hornet's nest?

But as soon as Wyles heard about Lily's condition, his attitude changed – from annoyance to absolute delight. This was fantastic news! That very morning, on Breakfast TV, a completely different couple – aided and abetted by him, of course – had told the world about CalmerCeutical's new wonder drug. Now, a *completely different* couple were having a baby because of it! How lucky can a pharmaceutical company get! You just can't *buy* PR like this!

He didn't explain this angle to Dr Taylor, of course. But what he did he tell him was that he'd send a consignment of Pheroxosol around immediately. They could have a truckload for all he cared!

Oh yes, and of course the other thing William Wyles *didn't* tell Dr Taylor was that as soon as he put the phone down he'd be straight on the phone to the tabloids. Add Ben and Lily's story to Francine and Johnny's story and bingo! He could see the headlines now: *Love Drug Pair To Have Baby*.

Of course, William Wyles' acquiescence surprised Dr Taylor. He was expecting far more resistance. Oh well, he thought. It just goes to reinforce what he'd always thought. If you tread carefully and logically, things always sort themselves out.

So as Wyles' babbled away, Dr Taylor scanned his computer for the trial's data. He'd need to email Amraj, CalmerCeutical's CSO, with the couple's prescription details.

At this point, all Ben and Lily could see was the back of a computer screen whilst Dr Taylor squinted at it – phone in one hand, mouse in the other.

Then, suddenly, the doctor sat bolt upright. His face had completely changed – part amazement, part amusement.

'Erm, William, I've come across something rather interesting.'

'What's that?' asked Wyles.

Just before replying, he spun his computer screen half-round and beckoned Ben and Lily to lean forward and look at it. On the screen was a table with the trialists's names on it. Next to these were rows of little ticked boxes indicating the dates when the drugs had been administered. Against Ben's name, and further down the list, against Lily's, was a continuous row of 'P's.

'What do they mean?' asked Ben.

'Placebos,' grinned the doctor. 'You've both been on placebos.'

They looked at the screen in disbelief. Placebos! All along, just placebos!

Then Ben looked at Lily. And then Lily looked at Ben and, in unison, a tiny smile crept across their lips. There was also, just, the possibly a tear in Lily's eye. They were just a normal couple. Well, sort of.

Dr Taylor gave them their moment. Allowed them their shared look, then turned the computer screen back and put the phone back to his ear: 'Er, Willian, are you still there?'

'Yes.'

'Well, it, er, does rather change things, doesn't it?'

'Er, yes,' sighed Wyles, 'I suppose it does.' He tried hard to disguise his disappointment, adding: 'Erm, while you've got that data up, you wouldn't mind telling me who else was on placebos?'

'Of course, no problem, er, let me see.'

He ran his eyes down the screen.

'Yes. It was Francine Smith and er… yes, Johnny O'Neill.'

'They're the four. The twenty percent.'

On the far end of the phone, the CEO's face whitened.

With the doctor's conversation now sounding as if the accusations were coming from the opposite direction, Ben and Lily gestured their goodbyes, got to their feet and left.

They linked arms and, laughing, walked back down the corridors – past wards, common rooms, cafés – that had, some six months earlier, changed their lives forever. Eventually they got to the reception area, where they said a brief farewell to Nurse Angela.

Arm-in-arm, they strolled past St Thomas's, past County Hall and along the South Bank.

They de-linked and started to walk up the steps to Hungerford Bridge.

'So,' said Ben, 'It wasn't down to chemicals after all.'

'Oh, yes it was,' said Lily, 'It's just that they were ours.'

'Are,' said Ben, as they reached the top, '*Are*.'

And there they stood. Two people, silhouetted against a Waterloo sunset, in love. Well, sort of.

Ben & Lily & ...

'Hi love, how's it going?' asked Lily, taking off her coat. 'Not bad, I suppose,' said Ben, getting up from his laptop. 'Can't quite see how it's going to end though.'

'Right,' said Lily absentmindedly, making for the sofa.

'I'll, er, make a cup of tea... how was work?'

'Oh, so, so.'

They'd got into some kind of rhythm. Every day, Lily, her bump now properly showing, would go off to work, leaving Ben to, well, do all the things that she didn't – a bit of housework, some cheap food shopping, an evening meal from the scraps he'd just bought. Oh yes, and on Thursdays, he looked in at the Job Centre, which was depressing, but mandatory.

There was work out there, but not the kind he was accustomed to. Accustomed to? What, he increasing asked himself, made him so bloody special? Bermondsey born and totally uneducated – what was wrong with flipping burgers or stacking shelves? This was 2012 for fuckssake! Anyway, he'd have to do something soon. Lily's job would be finishing in a few months and the only other income they had – the surplus rent from his highly mortgaged flat – hardly counted.

'Spoke to Mum today,' said Lily, leaning back, taking the weight off her feet.

'Oh yes, how is she?'

'Oh fine. They're coming over on Sunday. Got loads of stuff, apparently: Moses baskets, baby-grows, you name it.'

Her parents had been terrific. Non-judgmental, supportive, generous. There was even the possibility, come the time, they'd move in with them until they'd sorted themselves out. Even if Ben did find work in central London, Beckenham was just as commutable as Lewisham.

'Great,' he said, squeezing a second cup out of a single teabag.

'So what were you saying about the end?'

'End?'

'The story.'

'Oh right, yeah…'

He put the teas on the table in front of her, sat down and gave her a kiss.

Since moving back in with Lily, there had been two other activities taking up his days. The jogging, he still did: Hilly Fields, Blackheath, even Greenwich. His running, like Lily's tummy, was ever growing. The way he saw it was, being unemployed, he had to keep himself active, both mentally and physically – and the running covered the latter. The former? Well, he was writing a book. It was all about a boy who starts with nothing, becomes a big shot and then, *possibly*, ends with nothing again – he wasn't even halfway through it and still wasn't fully decided about that bit. It would probably never be published anyway. But he did kind of enjoy writing – it was therapeutic, he said.

Either way, Lily approved and helped him here and there. Sitting together, going over his writing, it took her mind off things too. Things? The permanent tiredness, the intermittent sickness, the everything. And even if some of these symptoms did diminish, they'd be replaced by others. Life certainly wouldn't be getting any easier over the coming months – or years, come to that.

So had she made the right decision? On balance… maybe. But that's the whole point – it was a balance. By now, had she taken the other road, she could have been anywhere: Bangkok, Beijing, Rio. Everyone wanted English. So did that mean she was unhappy? What a stupid question. It wasn't a case of happy or unhappy. It was a case of pregnant. And poor, come to that.

'So,' she said. 'Let's see what you've written.'

'Oh, right, yeah.'

He got up from the sofa and picked up his laptop. Suddenly, his normally silent phone chirped up, vibrating its way to the table edge. He put his laptop back down and picked it up.

'Hello... Yes, it's Ben here ... Right... Really? Are you sure? Sorry, I mean... it's, er, some time since... But I thought I wasn't... I see, right... I'll, er... Okay... right, good...

Yes, thanks.'

Almost dazed, he put the phone back down.

'Who was that?' asked Lily.

'Nothing.'

'Nothing?'

'As in the company.'

'What did they want?'

'Me... I've got the job.'

'You've... that's... that's *terrific*!' said Lily.

She would have jumped to her feet and kissed him if she didn't feel so shattered. Sudden images: Ben's big beautiful flat and designer baby buggies, al fresco coffee shops and yummy mummy gatherings.

'Yes,' he said. 'Yes, it is.'

Lily then frowned slightly: 'They took their time, didn't they? I mean, that must've been... well, almost three months ago!'

'Yeah. Some bullshit about lots of applicants – and waiting for this new account.'

'So you, er, think they had someone else in mind... originally, I mean?'

'Definitely,' he said, sitting himself back down next to her. 'I mean, as a rule, no one gets back to you in this business, but that's obviously bollocks.'

She thought for a second, put her hand on his knee and said: 'You don't sound very pleased, Ben.'

'No, no... I am, honestly.'

Lily then said: 'Hang on a minute. I thought you said you were awful. You know, at the interview?'

'Yes, they even had an answer to that – well, implied one. He said that's why I got it.'

'That's why you got it?'

'Yes, because I was crap. Because I said nothing. He thought I was being ironic – or so he said. They love that fucking word – in advertising, I mean.'

Ben then flickered a little smile at her. Memories were flooding back for him too.

'So you are... I mean, you are going to take it, aren't you?'

He sighed, looked down at his fingers and said: 'Yes, I guess so.'

'Look, Ben, you mustn't feel you have to.' Her hand was still on his knee.

He looked back at her, smiled and thought for a second. Then he gave her a little kiss and said: 'Well, Lily... it's better than nothing.'

Lily

Ben had the first words, so I suppose I might as well have the last.

How did it all end up? Well, Ben did work for Nothing, still does, though not in the monetary sense, obviously. Does he like it? No, not really, but that's life. He has this little theory about it. Says Nothing's well named because that's what his job is. He told me that the only thing that makes it *something* is Alfie and I – which is sweet. Mind you, he then went and spoilt it all by saying something about his job being fucked and the only thing that *stopped* it being fucked was *knowing* that it was fucked – which I can't say I fully understood.

He's changed a lot, you know. He's had to. But I hope I've changed a little bit too. You see, I was pretty judgmental back then, wasn't I. Remember my first thoughts? When I saw him, I mean: 'Quite a contortionist: through a hedge backwards *and* up his own arse.'

And did we go back to his lovely Stoke Newington flat? Yes, but now we're thinking of moving back to South London. It may seem strange, but we've got fond memories of the area where we first lived together. Blackheath or Greenwich would be perfect. Oh yes, and that reminds me. If you're worrying about McFlurry, don't. He had about three different flats on the go, and he soon shacked up with the old woman down the corridor.

So why are we moving so soon? South of the river you get slightly more for your money – space-wise, I mean. Very soon, little Alfie will have a brother or a sister. And that's another reason it would be good to move back. I'm going to need a little more help now. Nearer the grandparents, you see.

You know, one way or another, like it or not, we're all under the influence of something. Family, eh?